InstaFall of U.S.A.

BY BEN COMPANI

DORRANCE
PUBLISHING CO
EST. 1920
PITTSBURGH, PENNSYLVANIA 15238

Dorrance Publishing Co
585 Alpha Drive
Pittsburgh, PA 15238
Visit our website at *www.dorrancebookstore.com*

ISBN: 978-1-6366-1216-4
eISBN: 978-1-6366-1806-7

InstaFall of U.S.A.

DNA Never Admit That You Killed

A Classic Science Fiction Mystery

Our Flawed and Primitive DNA

Can 5 Viruses Unify U.S.A.?

Communism VS Capitalism

Highly Entertaining and Informative

National Security, Virus, Thrill, Science, Fiction

Dedicated to my beloved family.

Table of Contents

Introduction

A few words to my dear reader:
I am honored that you have bought my book and are sharing a few hours of your precious life with me, traveling through this fascinating science fiction journey. I assure you that the journey will be a thrilling one, full of excitement, fear, passion, anger, despair and fulfillment. If you have a heart condition, I suggest that you do not continue reading this exciting play. It is a play of our Universe.

To the best I could, I have written this book in a common man's language, though on occasions I had no choice but to use some scientific terms. This is not only a science fiction mystery book. It engages us in some philosophical debates. Hopefully together we will learn new scientific facts about life, from the beginning to the future of our Universe and our place in it...or better to say the Universe's place in us. Even though in a relational world there is really no difference between the two. As you know better than I do, we are entangled with the natural world. There is no separation. There is no sound of one hand clapping. There cannot be a Ping Pong unless there are two players and a stage. You give a Ping to the Universe, the Universe will give you a Pong back in return, all in a stage that we call curved Space-time with its many quantum fields. It is a Wholesome One.

During our journey we will engage in and debate about existence or non-existence of a deity, the negative and positive power of "Prayers," and whether we have or exercise what is so casually called "Freewill," which I believe is a total misnomer.

As you read this book, you and I will emotionally move together. Your hormonal activities will go up and down. You will notice changes in your brain… some temporary and some permanent. We know that our lives are made up of short stories, of many experiments, moments, events, failures and successes. It is these short stories…the days and the years, that when added up, make up your life and mine.

With its ingredients, our Universe has made each one of us unique…to the extent that without you, the Universe would not and could not possibly exist the way it is. You are that unique. Your uniqueness comes from the fact that you, or better to say your ingredients, are the only ones that traveled through your many specific dimensional space-time pathways to get here. No other entity had that chance. They had their own unique way as well.

As you go through this fascinating book, I ask you not to be just a reader, but a feeler and an actor. While reading this play, your brain will be shattered then reassembled in many ways. New neuronal networks will develop and some of your old networks will be reactivated, hopefully for the better. You may remember some of your old, faded memories.

There are many players who will play their respective roles in this lively theatre. You will meet many of them right from the first pages, or as they enter this exciting journey…this theater. There are many players, and even strangers, in our real lives that we will never ever meet. Sometimes their effect on shaping our lives are much more drastic than the effect on us by our closest family and friends. I can only name a few of our players here without telling you their roles. Only their first names for now.

Akofa, William, Scotty, Marsha, Innocenti, Maria, Buzz, Mary, Charles, TC, Nikola, Elon, Po, and Dwight, to just name a few of them.

The focal point of the book is for us to find the mystery killer…or killers. We will also do our best for the world to avoid a major biological war between the United States and the country of Chima. Let's hope that you and I will succeed in avoiding that war. Even if we did avoid it this time, the dangers for the future will remain, as Chima takes over the United States of America to become the sole superpower. Will Chima end the status of the U.S.A. and the Western democratic countries? We may find out, or just give it our best guess.

Have no doubt…you and I will be emotionally engaged throughout this once in a lifetime journey. You…the reader and I…the writer will move around, hand in hand, mind in mind, going through this science fiction play. We will have many friends or enemies in this book. I have already named a few of them for you and you will get a feel for the very unusual and unique characters as you are reading the story.

Even though this is a thrilling science fiction book, I have no doubt that it will quickly become the subject of a science fiction movie. Mostly, a thrilling science education movie that will show the possible future of the U.S. and its role on our lively "Red Planet" we call home, our planet Earth. So hang on to your book if it is in printed form.

To find the killer, or killers, you and I will do what is called a "Quantum Jump." We will simply disappear and reappear wherever we desire. Our jumps will be void of any transition with nothing in between. You disappear and then reappear somewhere else, or in different times. We may have to violate some laws of physics, if we can even call it a violation. Since the people whom we will be visiting do not know they are being visited in their most sacred places, their minds, their homes or offices, we will be acting like "Quantum Spies." This is the only way we can solve our science fiction mystery.

So whenever you see a "Quantum Jump" it means we are ready to disappear and reappear somewhere else...anywhere or anytime. It could be in the past or in the future, in someone's neuron, cell, organ, or anywhere in the body. It could be in their emails, homes, military bases, or anywhere we need to visit to solve our mystery.

Our fictional visits or references may include the most secret places within the government, in the United States; including the Pentagon, the White House, the President's brain, the Congressional offices, and even the brain of some of our "not so sharp Representatives and Senators."

We may Quantum Jump to some secret places overseas, in country of Rubbas, the central government of the People's Republic of Chima and Chima's CDC. To solve our murder mystery, we may visit their military operations and study their long-term goals, including Chima's and Rubbas's highly advanced maneuverable satellites and most dangerous places such as Chima's advanced and mysterious biological labs.

There are two things that you will not know until the end of the book: Who the real killer was, if there was one or two, and one more secret that I cannot tell you right now. This book will teach you to have patience, so simply read on.

This is not just another regular book; it is different as you will soon realize.

Please understand that this is not a medical book, so do not consider my comments or suggestions as medical advice. This is not intended to be a national security book either…but who knows…maybe many points here will bring out our weaknesses as it relates to our national security.

Let us start if you are ready. I am. The thrill of our Universal Play starts here and now.

Chapter 1

William, Grace Ann and Akofa

"Honey something strange happened to me today," William told his wife Grace Ann.

"What happened hun?"

"Funny but very strange,"

"I was sitting in this park, looking old at my age of 95 with long white hair and white long beard, a couple of younger people thought that I am a wise guy...so they came and sat next to me on the bench for a few minutes. They were asking me to advise them...especially about their relationship with their wives or girlfriends...as if I know it all. Well, we have been married for 75 years. So maybe you and I have done something right,"

"Suddenly this different looking person came and sat next to me. He looked so different...had bigger eyes and was taller and his eyes were neon blue and his skin a bit light neon green. Since it is close to Halloween I thought he had made changes to his appearance, or maybe he is just one of those crazy guys. But then he started indicating with some kinds of gestures...like a sign language, trying to tell me something. I paid attention trying to understand his gestures, but did not fully understand what he was saying, was he not capable of talking or was he deaf? But indications were that he wanted to put a puck looking small round shaped thing on my head. I showed him my phone and with the same kind of gesture tried to indicate that I had to use my phone, he shook his head meaning ok go ahead and that is when I called you to let you know that I was going to be late. So I did not reject his offer with my gestures as if it would be ok for him to put that little thing on my head and he did. What the heck I told myself. I'll let this guy have some fun with me and nothing will happen to me I thought. So I started some kind of engagement with him after he put the little round thing on my head,"

"I know hun, I started getting worried when you called but I did not press it. So what happened? Did he put that thing on your head? Are you now crazier or wiser? I don't want anyone to bother my man," Grace Ann told William.

"Yes he did, and he said that he had come from another planet and has been here for a few days. I realized he was definitely playing games with me and I did not want to be playing his childish game; I need to get away from him, I don't have time to waste here. So I gave the little round thing back to him, stood up and walked away, but he got up and followed me. I walked faster and he did the same and caught up with me. He came next to me and said in good English, 'Please believe me, I have come here from another planet and want to share with you, my intention is to help your species.' So we got to another bench and we sat down,"

"I felt some kind of activity in my brain. He told me that he had downloaded our language from my brain to his brain. How ridiculous, I thought...the man must be crazy. Yet I was understanding him perfectly and we started conversing,"

"He said that the planet he had come from is located in our Milky Way, by the name of Zafeera. He told me that we could not physically go there because of my body's limitation going in a fast moving spaceship. Because of what he put on my head, he told me that in a few minutes I would start imagining that I am on their planet and experience the events unfolding, just as if I was on planet Zafeera. He said that I could see and experience things and converse with their inhabitants in English. He mentioned that I could not talk in their language of course, because my brain cannot physically make rapid changes to understand another language. All of a sudden, I had a strange feeling as if I were in a different, very advanced planet with him...as if a movie started running in my brain. Everything looked so advanced...a totally different surrounding. He told me that my brain had become somewhat an extension of his brain and he said his brain's operation at the neuronal level is quantumly entangled with his planet Zekta brain,"

"I was being greeted by people who looked like us, except they had longer ears and bigger blue neon eyes. Their color skin was a bit neon light green, and they all were the same size, about 5 inches taller than me, no difference from one another in their skin color,"

"The inhabitants were the friendliest creatures you would ever desire to meet. It appeared that there were no other animals on their planet...just creatures like him. No children either. Everyone appeared to be at the same age...happy as hell...same size...and they appeared like they only had one sex,"

"I asked him if they were biological beings and he said they were. He said that they have been studying us for thousands of years, but this is his first trip here,"

"This felt so real, I could not imagine that I was dreaming, so I started asking him some questions about their way of life,"

"Do you guys die like we do?" I asked.

"No, we decide to go to long sleeps until we and our Zekta brain decides to wake us up. We go to special places and sleep there. We still need some energy you know, even when we sleep. Just like yours, our life has a purpose. We are complex beings and like you, our biology works like yours...just differently," He replied.

"You referred to a Zekta brain...what is that?"

"I will explain it to you later," he said.

"How differently are you from us," I asked.

"He said he can explain their main characteristics. They are biological beings... they eat...they are carbon based biologically...they dispose differently because their food is in extremely condensed forms...they do not have children the way we do. They give their special cell to a machine and provide detail characteristics and the machine produces an individual just like their size, but they are their children, and they are not allowed to have more than two,"

"Our feelings toward our children are just like yours. The children grow, but only grow mentally...not physically, since they are physically born the same size as others. We are bionic beings...biologically driven, but with many gadgets and outside circuits with technology, especially mentally. Our ancestor, who created the Zekta brain, did not see any ethical violation performing genetic engineering since it was species driven. Our individual body works on a biological basis, but with external help. We have access to extra memory outside of our body. Body parts are reproducible outside of us...so we don't die...we just intentionally go to sleep,"

"We regenerate limbs or internal organs in our engineering labs using our pluripotent stem cells. You may think we are creepy, but we are augmented beings with different very advanced DNAs, millions of years ahead of yours,"

"Because we have redesigned our body, you can think of us as Trans-human. We took the genetic lottery and probabilities out of our DNA's replicating power. We are all connected in purpose through input and output from our big brain. There are many chips and artificial intelligence involved in our bodily functions and connections. Psychology has less meaning for us than for you,"

"We don't blame you for the way you are...you are just born and grow differently compared to us. We are the intelligent life that you are looking for or become of. Learn from us to accelerate your evolutionary process since your DNA is flawed, primitive and underdeveloped,"

"Our DNA is not short like yours...it is 200 times longer, but we got rid of some of its junk. We have combo genes that you don't and that makes us much smarter and gives us a much faster brain and genetic power. Our genes, in comparison to yours are like the instruction coming from a word, a sentence, a book and an encyclopedia. Some of our combo genes are like encyclopedia, some are like books and some sentences, we have combo genes and you don't. Just like you, our lives are purposeful. We have a dynamic living system and our life molecules are homochiral. We don't grow outwardly, but we evolve internally. We have homeostasis and process energy just like you do, but we do it differently, extremely efficient and not much waste,"

"My host told me that on this planet there was no killing, no lying, no cheating, and no stress of any kind. I was meeting the kindest people you ever desired in the cleanest, relaxed and advanced environment. I really didn't know if this was a dream or if it was real. The light coming from their Sun felt differently...a bit warmer and much brighter. Apparently no or very little pollution,"

"My host asked me if I wanted to look at how they were developed and how we as humans act in a particular cut of time. He took me to a huge indoor arena. This arena was a special four-dimensional arena. I could see everything in three dimensions, but also had time as the fourth dimension. He told me that we can sit here and select a year and look at life on Earth on a real time basis. We could Quantum Jump to different places,"

"This is how we changed. Our many, many generations past had realized the inadequacy of their brain and how aggressiveness had caused them agony, killing, and lack of happiness. Millions of years ago our species made some big decisions. They knew fighting was destructive for their species, so they had decided to make their brain a collective brain. They were already very technologically advanced. They had studied millions of people in huge Artificially Intelligent machines connected to 10,000 fMRI machines to see what the real causes of their mental ills were. They studied the minds of millions of normal, mean, happiest and saddest people. They realized that collective brains were more stable and friendlier than those of each individual brain acting disjointed and on their own,"

"Using their advanced AI machines, our ancestors had come up with a species focused approach as to what a collective brain should think and how it should function. Being biologically advanced creatures, they started a big biological brain project, assembling it one neuron at a time...a very long process. It took them thousands of years to build this Zekta brain. Imagine it is like a million brains combined in one. Then their genetic engineering took over and made us who we are today. One of our differences with you all is our looks, because our sun is different than yours and our gravity is different. We have delegated many of our big decisions to this Zekta brain. We had learned that a single neuron works on probabilities and can act irrationally, but a few neurons jointly act on a more stable basis, so connecting these into a bigger brain...like the human brain makes it even more stable. But the difference is that our big brain connects with all of our twenty billion brains giving and receiving feedback. You can imagine how stable this huge interactive operation would be with less rash decisions. It protects all of us at the brain level. There are twenty billion of us with one species driven purpose and we have become an extremely stable species. Our immune system is so strong that we do not worry about viruses and bacteria , our combo genes are a part of our bodily defense, of course the atmospheric condition of our planet also helped with that,"

"One of our ancestors' main intentions was to get rid of making rash decisions and consequences of illogical mental actions and reactions. They studied many people in their family settings, then in their cities and in their nations. The same meanest individuals were acting so differently in a group setting. The AI machines were studying them. The collective brain was acting much calmer and with thoughtful action not rash or mean decisions. The killings started to diminish,"

"So little by little millions of people had agreed to join this project and finally we became one conscious species. Our ancestors knew that they had to deal with the functioning of the brain...no metaphysics. They were serious in their objective since it was for the survival of our species. We knew that even as an individual totally isolated from the society, we retained our intellectual imprint. Our species had to come up with a collective mind, a collective consciousness, as their main mode of functioning. If our freewill was to help our species, we had to delegate it to and accept the notion of collective intentionality. We had given up much of our freewill to Zekta brain. It took us hundreds of thousands of years to do this. Not easy, but achievable. This is not the same equivalent as electing leaders. Leaders still use their own intent, sometimes more moderated decisions, but sometime extremely irrational ones. This is collective decision making. Our species rejected this approach for generations but realized the benefits of shared brains. They started downloading their preferences and many other significant decisions into this big collective brain. It is still cognitive science. The AI machines are an extension of our minds. It became like a shared external mental state for our own brains,"

"We make our day to day decisions, but not the big decisions that affect our species. Economic and production decisions are made by AI machines connected to Zekta brain. We also give and receive constant biofeedback with Zekta,"

"Cars, transportation, manufacturing and distributions are all automated. Our mental joy is different than yours and our consciousness is at a much higher level since our brains are devoid of fear, of death and killings. We have been watching you for the past fifty thousand years. You are not at fault...this is how DNA evolves...slow and conservative. It can become very advanced, but it will take millions of years. Our species had realized the limits of our biological capacity. We do visit and explore a few other planets with our blazingly hyper fast spaceships. We still have limitations but are working on them with our collective brain,"

"We can see your human brain and what is happening in it in terms of thinking. We are cybernetic beings and our societies use an advanced form of logic, unlike your primitive logic. We found and eliminated senseless violence as a start. This is not in a realm of fiction, so we have scientists of all kinds...astrophysicist, biologists, and biological anthropologists...our educational system is very advanced. Our mathematical power and understanding of the physical world at the chemical, subatomic, and biological level is much more advanced than yours,"

"You have to start with big vision for your species. I know it may look like an immense complexity on the surface, but you can start with setting simple goals. Don't waste your resources...expand on it with technology. We have become a very advanced biological, digital society. Unfortunately, in your case, your behavior is hardwired by your DNA and it gives it limitations. It acts on an evolutionary basis, with individual goals at its center of attention...very selfish,"

"The Zekta brain actively guides us. There is a fundamental unity between the gigantic Zekta brain and each one of our inhabitants because the base architecture and computational power of the Zekta and ours is the same. They are tightly linked. We used anthropology when designing the architecture of the Zekta brain, with input from all of our planet's inhabitants. There is no contemporaneous silence or inaction between our brain and the big one. It is a constant inflow and outflow between them,"

"The vast collection of neural network and interactions gave us the roadmap for our complex social order. We transformed and combined the intention of our inhabitants...not an easy task. Our ethical dimensions are species centric, with the whole assembly morphed one neuron added to another, one at a time,"

Our individual brains have such a close, augmented, intelligent connection with the Zekta brain. We are so happy that a few million years ago our ancestors recognized the necessity of rethinking our intimacy between the inhabitants and Zekta brain, we are a happy species as a result. We feel we are one, and not two separate beings. We dance together and enjoy the living brainy side together. The big brain is alive with consciousness. It has its own personality and identity...it cannot talk but it feels pain and pleasure just like we do. Its organic and nonorganic parts work hand in hand as they have been fused together. You guys have to reset many of your behavioral habits and let it unfold on a species-centric focus,"

"You will find tools for your transformation like we did. To you, we are extraterrestrial, but we don't look at ourselves like that. We have used and exploited our environment to support our cognitive power. They are like external mental states as an extension of our brain. We have collective intelligence much more powerful than the sum of the individuals...emergence of extra behavioral consciousness at a higher level did manifest itself. Even if the big brain's parts fail us...which it will...we still have our identity and will retain our intellectual imprint. However, don't look at our collective mind as a metaphysical entity,"

"The Zekta brain is being copied on a real time basis in many places and just in case it starts malfunctioning, it repairs itself biologically. Even if all big brains and back up fall apart, we are still a big society...calm and collective. Our DNA has been evolved for us to act like that,"

"Zekta has many auxiliary organs and they work on a somatic basis. Our bodies are half machine bionic with techno formic complexity and extrasomatic biological power. There is no concept of individuality and selfishness since everything is species-driven. Our individual input had a profound influence on the main structure of the big one. Life is strange, but we did not allow its philosophical dimensions to control the design of the big brain,"

"Make peace as your initial law, and give it a chance to develop into a bigger connected brain of your species,"

"We harness energy like your plants do, with much reserved energy for thousands of years. Our AI machines make economic decisions and we do not work, the machines do. They produce and distribute...we only think and transfer our needs to the big brain and enjoy happiness. We do not die, but we can stay in sleep mode forever or be destructed and reused by the collective action of Zekta brain,"

"Seeing how relaxed and happy they were, I quickly jumped on him with my question. I asked him if they had names,"

"No," he said. "Everyone is recognizable from their looks, even though we all look the same. Some kind of brain waves are recognizable, but call me Akofa,"

"I asked him what he sees and reads off my brain, and if he finds anything wrong with it,"

"Is your wife's name Grace Ann"? Akofa asked.

"I told him yes and asked him what my cell phone number is. He told me what it was. I wondered how he knew all of that. He could not tell me what our land line number was, so apparently, he did have some limited brain power, but maybe because I did not remember it myself. Being a math professor, I thought I should test him with a tough math question to solve. I brought it up on my iPad and showed him and he solved it in a blink of an eye. Then I asked him what he thought of our behavioral problems, as he saw them...compared to theirs,"

"Just look at your vocabulary. Look at what kind of garbage your DNA...through your brain...is generating. Your brain clearly tells me how primitive your DNA is...full of hate and anger. Our advanced DNA got rid of all selfishness and hate because they only hurt your collective mind,"

"Just look at what your primitive, and with my apologies if I can call it retarded DNA is coming up with...all these nasty, hateful, negative words. Words like....

> animosity, annoyance, antagonism, displeasure, disgust, fury, hate, impatience, jealousy, outrage, resentment, rape, rude, selfish, temper, violence, revenge, tantrum, ill temper...and many more,"

"Millions of years ago, our ancestors had them replaced with the more caring and loving words such as; love, devotion, fondness, friendship, passion, respect and enjoyment,"

"Our DNA is genetically engineered not to think any other way, at the end of the day it is your DNA that eventually creates your consciousness,"

"Compared to us you are like an infant who was just born and in its very first stages of development. Even the brain of your wisest, oldest man is like a newborn who is trying to find the first milk from the mother to survive and to learn spatially and temporally. You are in the infancy of your fight against extremities,"

"Biologically we are ten million years ahead of you, but don't feel bad. We feel your pain and anger, but unfortunately, they are a part of the process to get to where we are. Just like you...at your stage of development, we were not developed mentally except little by little as our species acted. We are now one species with a collective mind, but you are many, with billions of disconnected brains. Our brain...and especially the big brain's architecture and anthropology power is much more advanced,"

"We wished we could be of help to your species, but it is only you who collectively can make the necessary sacrifices to redirect your progress. It will take generations and millions of years to become one thinking species but have no doubt that you will get there. We can only give you advice as to how we got here. We succeeded but your neuronal network and your genes will take time to change. It may take hundreds of thousands of years, but let love prevail in the process,"

"Make innovations in understanding the effect of nature on your DNA as it takes its course, and it will save you just as it did for us. Your genes will be your destiny...if, and only if...everyone's genes are going to share their intent through sharing of thought. You will learn how to use Epigenetic power to your advantage. Your progress in genetic engineering is a start. Just be careful,"

"Our species was just like yours, but no more. We do not fight or destroy each other. We have changed our DNA not to and we have taken the aggression out of our nature and out of our souls and minds,"

"Have faith in yourselves with certainty of success. Try to become one neuronal network. Feel one another. Let the pain of others be the pain of the neuronal network. We went through the same process...the killing of a one another...nations against nations, gender against gender, and races against races, but it took us this long to overcome these ills...these senseless ills of the brain. You will too and time is on your side, as painful the process will be. This is not your fault. It is what it is for your species and it is a part of development."

"Let love be the foundation of becoming one big neuron. Let it be the root of your species evolutionary tree...a long, long journey with much pain to endure. Use what is above your head and under your feet, as they will help shape your DNA. Don't wait for any creator to give you love. Instead, let yourself to become the creator of passion,"

"Are you ready to look at what is going on your planet Earth? He asked.

"Yes, but can you change our future," I asked.

"Heck no," he said. "We don't and probably never will have that kind of power. We can only teach you, and it is you and your species who can shape your future?"

"I told him that I had to go to my wife. He said to take this device and put it on your wife's head for two minutes and to keep it as their gift to our human species. He said this is what is happening on our planet and to watch it with my wife," William explained.

"How long have you been married?" He asked.

"75 years," I replied.

"Great, we don't have marriages like you do," Akofa replied with a strange look on his face, his eyes popping out even more.

"So, honey let me put this little thing on your head and continue living our lives as humans. Let's watch our own story as it unfolds. Let's watch our planet Earth manifest its theatrical show,"

All of sudden they heard the doorbell and there was Akofa. He said he will live with them if they didn't mind, and he became their guest for some time. He had a much bigger device with him to continue regenerating his power. He said he may go to his Spaceship on and off to take care of his biological needs.

So here we go watching the stories unfolding on our planet Earth, somewhere in our tiny little Milky Way within our vast magnificent Universe. Let's cherish whatever it gives us.

Chapter 2

Innocenti and the Dream

Once upon a time, there was this man...a man of God named Innocenti. Innocenti Cristo. He was adopted and raised by an Italian family. He is a Priest, but his belief in God was constantly changing as if he is riding on a rollercoaster. His belief has been going up and down, left and right. But we should not prejudge this kind man until we hear him out and look at his life in more detail. Let us join Maria, his wife, and listen into the mind of this Godly man. Let us hear him out talking to his God. We will now take our first Quantum Jump and go right into Innocenti's brain.

"God, I have a big question for you...please be patient with me and give me a few minutes of your time. I know when I ask you my question you will not be able to give me a persuasive answer. You may get mad and burn me in your specially made oven...your Hell...just like your own creature Hitler did in Germany, burning thousands of Jews. He probably followed you as his example, who knows...maybe you were his idol, maybe he had read 'your' books.

God...if and only if, you are there and are listening, I have no choice but to level with you. After all, you know everything about me. You brought me here, in my unique universal travel path. Why in hell did you create me so dumb? Is it my dumbness that has attracted me to you? Don't laugh at me God...I am damn serious. I need a straight answer from you...don't gimme a bunch of garbage...be straight. If you don't have a good answer then go to your arsenal and kill me...don't give me the nonsense you have been giving to your creatures. Your standard answer when you are cornered is 'none of your business, I chose to do so.'

Listen to the words of one of your creatures portraying your characters…
His name is Richard Dawkins. He wrote a book about you called 'The God
Delusion.' To make it easier for you I will only quote a tiny part of his book
here. It is about you and your qualities. Let me summarize it for you…not to
take your precious time God…I know you are creating trillions of Universes
and don't have any time to waste. This is what he wrote about you…sad but
maybe you are to blame not Richard.

'arguably the most unpleasant character in all fiction, jealous and proud
of it: a petty, unjust, unforgiving control-freak; a vindictive, bloodthirsty
ethnic cleanser; a misogynistic, homophobic, racist, infanticidal, genocidal,
filicidal, pestilential, megalomaniacal, sadomasochistic, capriciously malev-
olent bully.'

Hey God, Richard probably ran out of bad words to show your character.
I can vouch that he is not your favorite creature or even a friend, will you burn
him when he comes to you? Or maybe you will love him because he did not
brown nose you. Did you help him write his book or did Richard write it on
his own after watching so many injustices in his lifetime? Maybe after watching
a red planet called Earth with so much biological killings in it…maybe he had
no other choice but to write it the way he honestly saw it. Hey God, are you
enjoying as you watch what is happening on this planet of ours…excuse me…
Your planet? Are you enjoying the rape, the killings, the hunger and the suf-
ferings in Africa? I think you are either enjoying it…or you are incapable to
stop it. Or maybe you just don't give a damn! Let me make a suggestion to
you God…next time…when you create another exoplanet like your Earth…
please make all 'humans' in one color…any color you choose…or with no
color. I kind of like navy blue. The way you created us with different colors
has caused so much grief, pain, and killings.

Please don't give me another nonsense…the so-called Freewill. What
Freewill, I ask you? Does a two-year-old innocent girl in Africa have the
Freewill needed to overcome disease, hunger, bacteria or fleas crawling all over
her? There are millions of these innocent kids! Are you kidding me with this
nonsense you call Freewill? We know that you cannot even talk or write to us
in a persuasive language. You have given us bunch of nonsense in your so-
called books of different religions, but…were you thinking…or are you even
capable of thinking when you supposedly wrote those books?

On the other hand, you have created many creatures who are nothing but love...they adore you and they love you...especially at good times. They say you are Omnipotent, Omniscient, and Omnipresent, but are these people kidding themselves or you really do have those powerful characteristics? If you do then why don't you use them, damn it? You have so kindly created us from the non-living and you have given us a one-time chance...the power to see, to hear, and to sense so many good things of your world. Couldn't you let only good things to exist and exclude the so painful ones?

Maybe the most honest ones among your creatures are those who say they don't want to judge you...because they don't see or hear you...they don't sense you...they don't know anything about you. After all, you have not proven yourself to anyone. You are just a self-declared powerful God. Nobody...I mean nobody...knows anything about you. Not a thing. They just assume you are there...somewhere...and each one of them assign you different good or bad traits. Why? I know why. Because you lack communication ability. And, God... don't dare telling me you chose not to communicate any other way...or you chose to let people guess about you. No more tricks please.

Just look at the way you have given us your 'books', inconsistent in themselves and between each other. You may not even be aware of this, but your books belittle your power. People are laughing at them...making fun of them...even burn them. Why? Because they contain so much nonsense. To make it mysterious, your Prophet goes up and disappears. People have to wait for his return...what return...when...till your hell freezes over?! Why are you playing this childish game of hide and seek with us, or maybe you got so bored and the only fun game for you was to explode yourself and are gathering yourself from the dust and pieces. Wake up God, wake up! Or maybe you are asleep and have put your Universe on an autopilot.

Your books cause fear in people and we know fearing is bad for their health. They have caused wars for decades...millions killed. Your books have fooled them into donating their hard-earned money to some thieves and criminals. Yeah...the money that really belongs to their children. They give their money to the so-called religious leaders...the billionaire Popes of the world... only because they fear you. Billions of dollars are spent to go around you portrayed as a 'stone' or bow to a 'wall' or they go to expensive buildings to see you. Why do they have to go to a bunch of thieves occupying expensive buildings to talk to you? Why can't they talk to you just like I am...for free. Maybe you pretend that you don't know why, but I do. It's because they have been told to do so from childhood. The thieves want to live luxurious lives on the back of the believers.

I have read your books...all of them. It looks like you can't even write. Are you the same God who wrote our DNA with this mega amount of information? Are you the same God who gave us the ability, through the same DNA the knowledge to edit our own DNA? Maybe your language is different. Maybe you talk to us using chemicals, neurotransmitters, or negative and positive charges. Are you the same all-powerful God who has created mega trillions of proteins in our body for us to be able to move...to think, to talk, to love? Are you the same God who is continually synching these proteins just for us to perform a function? I don't believe the same God who has written these books be the same power who has encrypted our DNA...it can't be.

Is this the way you express yourself by having our genes, a society of them, express themselves to make proteins, and therefore us? Gene expression is not an expression of kindness...or is it? Your Universe makes one little change in our DNA and our genes express so differently giving us conjoined twins, infant mortality and many other genetic diseases. You can't feel the pain because you are so powerful God. Maybe you don't know what pain is...maybe you can't feel it. I know...you only can create pain in others, right?

And we are not the only victims. For billions of years you did the same thing to other animals and creatures. They also expected you to be kind to them. Were you?

We have many good writers on 'your' planet Earth with clear understandable writing skill. If you need them to improve your communication ability to write your future books...to lead people to better places...and for them to be kinder, just let me know. I will find you a good skillful writer...of course free of charge God.

Your claim that you have given us the so called 'Freewill' is a bunch of nonsense. If we use our 'God given' Freewill and it does not correspond with your 'God's will' you will burn us, as you have promised in your ridiculously written books. Furthermore, you have made our 'Freewill' subject to so much randomness...controlled by electricity, ionic power and chemicals, or your so called epigenetic of the world. Is this how you delegate responsibility and power to others to 'freely' act? Utter nonsense! If they are free to act the way they choose why do you get mad at them? Just leave them alone…let them decide 'freely.'

But before I shut up, let me ask you my main question God…seriously…thanks for being so patient. I know you have plenty of time…maybe I am kidding myself. You own the time…you created the time. You created the elastic Spacetime, you created many interacting quantum fields. You are the one who created my brain…nobody else did. To create my brain, you had to savagely kill trillions of creatures before me to have my DNA evolved, right? You 'perfected' it with mutations to make it the way it is now. But you have created my brain with limited capacity to understand you. You have created me unable to understand the meaning of what is meant by the concept of 'greatest.' I can only understand what 'great' is and what 'greater' is, but my dumb brain does not have the capacity or capability to understand what the 'greatest' is. It always looks for a 'bigger' or a 'better.' And this brings me to my question, and I will anxiously await your answer my dear God, here it is:

How do I know you are 'the greatest'? How do I know that there is not another God better or bigger and more powerful over and above you? Another bigger God who even created you. I hope that by now you really see what our problem is. Our brain does not have the ability to understand the concept of what it means to be the 'greatest'. It always wants to look for something bigger, better, kinder, meaner or gentler than the 'greatest' and we will never achieve that…at least not with my limited brain.

Hey God, to summarize what I think about you…I wrote a poem for you. Here it is…I hope you enjoy it.

'Once upon a time orders came from God above
Mixed with seeds of hate and love
Confusing messages of love and hate
Turned love to hate at her Pearly Gate
Hey God please beware, if you dare
Remove their pain, give them some glare
If you scare them with hellish fear
Stress will make humans disappear
If you are there and I sincerely doubt

Be kinder, gentler, we don't need any doubt
This mess cannot be ordained from a loving God
God or Dog makes no difference, I am not awed
Either take charge or give us a loving brain
This brain is not the solution, it gives us pain
Having seen so much love and hate
You must be drunk or not awake
I hope you take a lesson from this little one
Take charge of your mess and make us a wholesome one'

"Hey, hey wake up Innocenti, have you been dreaming again? You have been talking to yourself for over fifteen minutes. Who were you talking to silly man? I told you not to take more than one of your sleeping pills. I told you not to read these biology and religious books, but you just don't listen to me. You have been talking and screaming. Since you were being so funny I did not want to wake you up," Maria told Innocenti.

So Innocenti wakes up more confused than ever, sweating like crazy. We think he was having a very scary dream.

Chapter 3
Scotty and Marsha

"Marsha honey, I have been an attorney for good many years…believe me I am about to give up. I am so sick and tired of this life dealing with other people's problems and our court system…especially when I don't see much justice being served," Scotty said.

"Scotty you know, as a practicing accountant my situation is no different than yours. I have to deal with our crazy tax system and the IRS, which is probably worse than dealing with your court system. I am sick and tired of my work too, and the sad part is that I see people suffer so much going through compliance with these nonsensical tax laws," Marsha said.

"Both of us are so stressed out, and medically we are being screwed without even realizing it," Scotty said.

"Yes, my love, but the problem is that we are not rich. We have some money in our account, but do we have enough to live on if we quit our practices?" Marsha asked.

"We are not that old to quit, but are you suggesting that we both quit working and retire? Let's talk about it later, but I am almost ready for that. We need to get away from this stress," Scotty told Marsha and continued.

"I will never forget the day that I was defending this innocent man who was charged with racketeering. A nice man. I knew he was innocent, but he got convicted. The prosecutor was running for an office and pushed his conviction. He was later released when his conviction was reversed on an appeal. This kind, African American man admitted to the Judge that even though he had used marijuana on occasions he had never ever in his life stored his marijuana in his freezer. We were able to prove that he had been framed by the police. The Judge believed him over the policeman, who was later convicted. He had planted the marijuana in the man's freezer," Scotty finished his comment.

"Well honey those were legal cases you were involved with, but oh my goodness, I will never forget the stress this young couple went through when they could not prove their case and had to pay the IRS a whole bunch of money. In their case the husband's father had a stroke while he was living with them. His mother, who was also living with them had fractured ribs and had incurable cancer. This young couple had a small construction company... netted something like $30,000 for the year. They got a notice of audit from the IRS the same day when the wife found out that she was pregnant. Later they found out that they were twins! During their move from their old rotten shack house to a bit bigger house they lost all their receipts and could not prove their expenses. The IRS gave them a whopping $70,000 tax bill," Marsha told Scotty.

"Didn't you tell me Marsha that the lady delivered the twins at the IRS office headquarter during the audit?"

"She did," Marsha confirmed.

"I am sure these kinds of ridiculous audits have happened to so many people... the stress kills you and makes you sick," Scotty said.

"Of course, our crazy system only supports our Senators and Representatives and the special interest groups," Marsha commented.

"I read in a few books that the cost of maintaining our tax system is about 600 billion dollars a year...I mean every year. That is like a whopping 20% of the money they collect in taxes goes for collection effort...unbelievable," Scotty said so pessimistically.

"And these stupid Senators have the guts to tell us that they don't have enough money to run the government and have to borrow every damn year... and from country of Chima, our number one enemy. They take us and our children deeper into debt,"

"That money could be used to pay off our national debt every year or to be used for medical and biological research, or for defense purposes," Scotty said.

"I know Scotty. We select our representatives so casually to serve in our Congress and it is hurting us so badly. Maybe it is our own fault you know,"

"Marsha, it looks like people don't care anymore. They think when they file their tax return and get a refund that they are actually getting extra money from the government," "Scotty, I am so sick and tired of this life," "let's sell our house…let's move to the mountain side. Let's go way up there free of the nonsense of the city life down here. We will have no contacts with anyone anymore…just you and me. And if we ended up having a child we will raise him or her in a natural world and we will do home schooling," Marsha says.

"Kids?!" Scotty screamed, "I don't think so. You said we want to relax from now on. How can we relax with a baby around, and who is going to help us with the delivery? Especially that you don't want to have any contacts with the civilized world. who can afford raising a child anyway?" Scotty asks.

"Did you say getting away from this 'civilized' world? Do you really think this a civilized world with so much killings in it…lying, cheating and discrimination?" Marsha asked.

"I know Marsha, the world has become a strange place…look at how many people die every day in international conflicts…but I like your idea of moving somewhere far. I mean far away on top of a mountain somewhere. Let's come up with a plan," Scotty said.

So a year passed, Scotty and Marsha quit their practices, sold their house, also bought a do-it-yourself cabin kit and a good size barn kit and assembled their log cabin and the barn on a piece of land on the highest skirts of a mountain. Scotty was a good handy man and together they raised some ten sheep and a few cows, a few hundred chickens, two roosters and a couple of horses. Why two roosters for one hundred chickens? That is a good question, maybe a biological answer will satisfy us for now, or maybe the roosters' biology compares well with those of some Kings in the Middle East! Scotty and Marsha also built a good size veggie and flower garden.

Watching over their two roosters one morning:

"Honey, look at these two roosters fighting over sex and domination, bloodying each other, when they really have no other reasons to fight, plenty of food around. Just look at that bigger one…he is almost killing the smaller one. He is bigger and when you are bigger, stronger or wealthier you always have the upper hand. They are fighting over who should have sex with the hens. What is this sex desire that dominates our world? Could God not have made a different world in which sexual desires were not so dominant…causing so much grief, rape, and killings in the animal kingdom or even humans?" Marsha asked.

"Yes, but to find the reason you may have to look at the biology of men versus women. Unfortunately, men have millions of sperms at a time, and each one of those sperms yells, through hormones of course…get me out….get me out. And this outing desire which is really a bunch of sex hormones are so dominant that it turns some 'otherwise normal' men to go crazy and this desire in some men become the very cause of mental disorders…rapes and killings of innocent girls or boys. What a world you have created my dear Lord?" Scotty replied and continued.

"You know Marsha? When I think about us, the living creatures…we are like these flower bulbs in the ground, they come out once a year and then go back down under, and when their head or flower is out they send their fascinating scents into the atmosphere and color the world. Some of them even let their sperms fly out to find a female waiting for them. Some bulbs make their kids in the ground next to themselves. Some of them let their seeds fly out in parachutes as if they were designed to fly. They land whenever the chaotic wind randomly takes them to their mate. So much for their Freewill," Scotty surmised.

"You are right. Just like these flower bulbs we also have come out of the ground once and eventually we will go back to the loving Earth. You know Scotty…no one can fight the gravity. We will all succumb to it one day. Once we are gone most probably we will never come back. One chance and one chance only. But when we are out, we should only love each other and not hate," Marsha said.

"But look at the problems and challenges we go through…ups and downs…left and right, weaving through the challenges we face. Of course with some happy times, too. Marsha my love, do you believe in reincarnation?" Scotty asked.

"No, that is a whole bunch of nonsense. It is not even pseudoscience," Marsha replied.

"Yeah, I don't believe in that garbage either. I know of this man…supposedly a chemist with a PHD, who believed in that nonsense. The man was so crazy. He believed that this present life of his was his fourth life on Earth. In his first life he was a Judge in England. He told me that as a Judge he made some bad judgements and he is now paying for those mistakes in his current fourth life. The man was so mean, he caused marital problems for his two children, causing both to go through divorce with three children, planned it and implemented it, ruthless, may his God help him with Karma. All he cared and talked about was money, money, money. You may think if we come back to live again that we will be better than before...not this man. In this life he has acted as a SOB. Hopefully, his Karma is not beyond reparable. Hopefully, he will do better in his fifth life," Scotty said with a gleam in his eyes.

Scotty and Marsha were having so much fun on the hillside outside of the "material world" of the city life. Every day waking up with the sound of their roosters, the moo of the cows, and the singing of the mountain birds...each bird singing a Bach or Beethoven, calling for sex and desire to pass their genes and to have children of their own. For Scotty and Marsha, picking up wildflowers of many beautiful colors with sweet scents was so relaxing and fun. At night, the sound of the rain on the wooden cabin was so loving, the repetitive music of the crickets and frogs was creating something like theta waves putting Scotty and Marsha to sleep, as they were so lovingly holding on to one another.

Scotty was milking the cows and the sheep. He was also a good handyman tending to the maintenance needs of the cabin. He was a good mechanic fixing the old truck of theirs on occasions. It was an old off-roader truck he had bought a few years back. Scotty had been babying this old tanned truck, and it was running like a clock. Even though the paint was peeling off on some spots, you could tell the engine and the transmission of the truck were the happiest parts in it.

"Honey...I have not had my period for two months, I think I am..." Marsha had not finished her sentence when Scotty jumped up and screamed.

"Oh my God, don't tell me you are pregnant...we can't afford raising a child here,"

"Wow, I thought this would be a good and exciting news for you sweetheart, but you seem a bit upset. Calm down Scotty," Marsha said, trying to hide her irritation.

"Oh no...I welcome the news honey and I thank our Lord for it, really... thank you God," Scotty mused.

Well, Marsha was pregnant, and you could tell that the belly was growing out as time passed. The morning sickness was sometimes unbearable for her, but no other choice...she had to tolerate it. A few months passed.

"Marsha, let me touch your belly sweetie pie.... oh my god...I think we have a set of twins; I feel their kicking, they are kicking as if they are in a soccer field," Scotty said, soccer being his favorite sport.

"What do you think they are feeling or thinking? Do they know what is out here? For sure they can feel and hear us," Marsha said.

Marsha and Scotty had a very relaxing life enjoying their mountain top cabin, they ate good food, went to the local farmers market at times, grew vegetables of all kinds in their own mountain garden, and were collecting eggs twice a day, keeping themselves healthy. We can only hope that their cholesterol is not shooting up with all these eggs and constantly drinking whole milk.

Scotty and Marsha were selling some of their vegetables, eggs and fruits in the local market along the Main Street and buying fresh vegetables of other farmers as they would stop to feel the skin of the watermelons and tomatoes. Everything was fresh coming from different nearby farms, all farmers and customers were talking in friendly ways and enjoying their time eating or sharing their grandma style homemade foods. You name it...they had it, from old time barbecue with special Cajun sauce to biscuits and peach cobbler and sweet tea. You could find plenty of finger licking food around these markets.

Life was so relaxing for Scotty and Marsha as they watched the cows looking around, half sleep, and chewing so lazily. There was much to learn from watching them. The beauty of patience...no rush. The birds were singing so nicely as their notes were streaking through the blue sky, trying to find a mate to have children of their own. A few more months passed.

"Marsha you are really getting big. Let me feel your tummy again and see how many legs we can find," Scotty said.

"I know I am kind of thinking maybe we have two little ones in there fighting... maybe twins...what do you think?" Marsha asked.

"No, the way your tummy is coming up I think there are six legs kicking but let me touch all sides of your belly. Nah, I think you are right and there are only four. When do you think the babies will come? It has been about 6 long months now?" Scotty asked.

"I don't know. You know as much as I do and I don't care, do you? Whenever it happens it will be fine with me, as long as the babies are healthy," Marsha replied.

"You know Marsha? Now that we know that we will have a set of twins, we need to talk about that to see if we should be raising them here or should we move back down to the city?" Scotty asked.

"No way, no way… no more city kind of living. We will do our best here and raise them to the best we can. Not everyone has to become an attorney or a doctor. They will be like countrymen producing real things like food for people," Marsha replied.

"I know Marsha. That was just a suggestion. Don't stress yourself out… you don't need any stress during pregnancy," Scotty said, trying to calm her.

"I know my love. I am getting so many kicks. You are right…it is like a soccer field in me…no refs though. They are kicking and kicking with no goalie. Every shot is a score," Marsha said smiling with the happiest face, but concerned about raising a child or two with little money and no serious help.

Marsha had taken a course in college about pregnancy and birthing, so she knew a little bit about the process of giving birth. But Scotty, no way…a scared chicken! Scotty and Marsha talked about the birthing process and decided to take their chances and believed they could manage the birthing and not go to a hospital. After all, giving birth is supposed to be a natural process. However, should they take this major risk? This is not Scotty's life that they are risking… it is the two little unborn lives and Marsha's life as well.

"Scotty let me tell you…a pregnant woman is the boss during birthing. Just be aware that in the brain of a pregnant women there are so many hormonal changes that make other parts of the brain…such as their frontal lobe…the neocortex to go dark and take the back seat and pretty much become inactive. Don't worry if I become rude, loud, whispering or even sounding sexy. I know I will hate light and noise. I will be overstimulated. I will for sure become moody and at times may even zone out," Marsha said, as she was teaching and warning Scotty, making him aware of her upcoming mood swings during delivery.

"And most importantly Scotty…I want to be assured by you, as the only person I love…that I will be safe and secure and that everything will go normal," Marsha finished looking for a confirmation look from Scotty.

"Of course my love. It is good that you had taken that college course on this, sweetie pie. You and I will handle it. I am here for you one hundred percent, so no worries," Scotty confirmed, but you could see him being so shaky inside.

They talked about the process of birthing some more, Marsha telling Scotty how it goes…in normal delivery of course…but will it be normal? Who knows? Marsha continued explaining the detail of the process from the moment the labor starts to the end where the umbilical cord must be cut.

"You know Scotty, we have to be careful with prolapse of the umbilical cord, it is a complication that can occur during delivery of the baby. The cord can come out ahead of the baby and can be trapped by the baby. It probably won't happen but just telling you in case it did," Marsha explained.

Every day they were blessed starting their day with a beautiful majestic sunshine, at times covered by mist or clouds. With the Sun's beautiful warmth and powerful force they were inspired as they walked early in the dawn, touching with their feet the dews on the mountain grass and picking some colorful wild poppy flowers to go in the vase, in the cabin.

"Marsha let me touch your tummy again…oh my god…they are kicking like they are mad…or maybe they are so happy thinking that they will come out of your belly soon," Scotty exclaimed.

"What do you think they are feeling or thinking? Do the kids know what is out here? For sure they can feel and hear us and share their inner language as they somehow communicate with each other. How do they know they have to look at our eyes when they are born and not at our hands? What is it about our eyes that fascinates them? Is it in our shared DNA? Hey Scotty, I feel a bit sad today. It is all about my hormones. Maybe it is my estrogen level causing it, I think," Marsha said.

"Yeah, it's probably just hormonal changes as you said," Scotty replied. But what did he know about hormonal changes?…he was just an attorney.

"To be honest with you Marsha, I am a bit sad today as well…when I think about our money situation I get stressed out. We don't have a whole bunch of money. Let me go to our town and sell that old small Persian rug, we have had it for a long time. It will be worth less if it rots," Scotty said.

"Ok hun go ahead. I was going to suggest that as well. Good thinking, you smart man. The kids are kicking hard again and with all their kicking I need to eat more. They need more food to grow healthy. Strange, when I sleep they go to sleep too. They act as if they are very considerate of me," Marsha said, happily.

So, Scotty goes to the small town and sells the rug for cash and comes back.

"Were you able to sell the rug honey?" Marsha asked.

"Yes dear, sold it for one grand! We will be ok for some time. You know it was a 90-year-old Persian antique," Scotty explained.

Scotty knew that they had spent all of their life savings when they bought the land and the log house.

"Marsha, you know that keeping children, especially twins comes with a lot of responsibilities…a long-term care and we do not wish to fail," Scotty said, with reluctance behind a brave face.

"What are you getting at hun? Why do you even have to mention it?" she asked.

"Marsha would you be upset if I make a suggestion dear?" Scotty asked.

"Well it all depends on what the suggestion is honey," Marsh replied.

"What if we use some of the money from the rug and go to see a doctor," Scotty said.

"Hey Scotty if you are even remotely thinking about abortion…no way… absolutely not. Oh God, these kids are kicking so hard. They are mad…maybe they heard you or felt your brain waves,"

"But Marsha we know we can't raise them here, no way, As we age it will be even harder. What if something happens to us? Who will take care of them? Adoption of course is another option. Marsha, think about it…it is serious. We were not really planning to have kids and I know that it was an accident, but we love them and have to be responsible as to how they will grow up here,"

"I know Scotty, I feel bad as well about how we can responsibly raise them here on the mountain top. Yes we did not plan to have kids but having a doctor to terminate their lives in a bloody scene…no way, no sir. We are not like those who irresponsibly have sex, get pregnant and after eight months they go and abort," Marsha said as she became emotional and started crying hard.

"Honey, don't cry, let's talk about our options and decide. I know your conviction and I respect that. I have seen you crying many times so silently… so I know you do not want to talk about abortion. I know we have other options. Like can we let our kids be adopted?"

Marsha and Scotty talked a lot about their situation as they were both very emotional and stressed and did not exactly know what to do, but finally decided to let the twins be adopted. They preferred for the children not to know that they have been adopted. They should let the adoptive parents decide when and how to let them know.

"You are the best Scotty. We are both mature and I think adoption is the most responsible way to go. You and I are so much the same the way we think. You are the best, most caring husband in the world. Promise you won't change your mind?" Marsha asked.

"Promise. Final, final," Scotty said.

Another month or two passed and the moment is now approaching. Any day now. How dangerous will it be?…no doctors and not even any midwifery help. They are taking a huge risk, especially having to deliver twins. It is a huge risk, not just for Marsha…but for the kids as well.

So, the moment has come and all the preparation and teaching by Marsha will hopefully payoff as Scotty and Marsha are getting ready to deliver the babies. Will it be normal? Is this chicken, Scotty, going to perform a C-Section?

"Oh God, these kids are so happy they are kicking as if they are playing the final championship. Maybe they are ready to jump out. They are tired of being there," Marsha said and continued. "Hey Scotty, I am a bit restless today and I feel a bit of contraction. I know you are here with me all the way aren't you? Please tell me everything will go normal," Marsha pleads.

"Of course honey. You and I will do the job…you take the lead hun, I noticed your breathing has changed a bit too and that is a good sign. Change your position now that you are on the bed. Always be ready. Lean forward hun and I am here waiting to see our two little ones coming to this world of ours, whenever they decide to come," Scotty encouraged.

The clock was ticking. A few hours passed. More stress, and finally after some 24 hours of laboring, early in the morning… as the Sun is coming up the kids are ready to enter their new world.

Scotty is delivering the babies …no one knows about them…no friends… just Scotty and Marsha sweating it out by themselves. They are on their own, but it was their decision. Finally, the exact moment has arrived.

"Push, push honey. You are doing so beautifully, you amaze me, you are so strong my love," Scotty was encouraging Marsha.

Marsha in full labor, screaming, sweating and pushing as she was pinching Scotty's arms and biting a towel.

"Oh my God, here comes the first one honey, you are doing such a good job, push, he is almost out I see it, I mean the little thing, your first little boy is born," Scotty said almost crying with joy, "We have a boy…we have a boy,"

Marsha push hun, I will cut the cord when the second one is out. Come on Marsha…exhale now, inhale, push, be strong you can do this,"

Scotty was out of breath. It is a bloody show…red all over…too much blood. Maybe something is going wrong, bleeding excessively can cause her to faint or even die.

Maybe we should have had a midwife here. What if this will be a breech birthing? No Caesarean section here, oh my Lord, Scotty is thinking. But too late to change the course.

"Push Marsha honey, the second one is almost out…maybe a girl, we will know shortly sweetheart. Marsha are you ok? Oh my God I think she is passing out…Oh my Lord, why is she not responding? Come on hun," Scotty urges.

The babies were born, looking healthy, but how about Marsha? Was she okay? Unfortunately, you and I will now have to leave Scotty and Marsha and do our Quantum Jump and go to the future and look at the life of one of those children many years later. Let's look at the life of Buzz. We will find out about his life and then rewind the world and come back to see if everything went well with the birthing. And what happened to Marsha…did she die? Were these children raised by just the father? Were they adopted?

Chapter 4

Buzz and Mary

Our Quantum Jump takes us to one of the children named Buzz, and his wife Mary.

Some 28 years has passed and one of the children is a grown up now. He is an engineer, chemist, a biologist and an astronaut, named Buzz Armstrong.

Buzz was adopted by a very caring family, who were all scientific. From childhood his adoptive father, Tommy Armstrong, a mechanical engineer specializing in avionics, was teaching him about flights, space and mechanics. Buzz's adoptive mother, Eugenia, was a biotech PhD and studied in Microbial Biotechnology. She was involved with how viruses are created and changed by forcing synthetic mutation. She had been studying the new field of Emergence, trying to study how life emerged from non-life. Unlike Tommy, who was mostly involved with non-life objects and gadgets, she was always occupying herself with studying life and human behavior and how non-life affected the behavior of the living creatures.

Having a father who was immersed in science caused Buzz to constantly read and write as he was growing up. Buzz was so smart, he finished high school at the age of 15 and went on to get his PhD in Aviation Technology. As an honor student, he followed up his studies in biotechnology.

Buzz was always interested in making small devices with tiniest actuators and the smallest electrical gadgets. Knowing chemistry, he used chemical reactions to engage and activate tiny devices.

Buzz became an astronaut at the age of 28 and went on different missions in the International Space Station. He did a few space walks and he also did a few repair jobs on satellites. He was given serious studies related to radar activated modules with a reach of thousands of miles activating devices on Earth. He was given some major studies in Neurology and brain networking dealing with seizures.

With an estimated 100 billion neurons in our brain and trillions of dendrites, studying neural pathways required not only great amount of knowledge in neuroscience, but a great amount of memory. For him it was an enjoyable field.

Buzz wrote many scientific articles and published many books. He became internationally well known in different scientific fields. He studied the brain of London and New York taxi drivers and how memory forms in some birds. Taxi drivers have a strong memory as their hippocampus in their brain gets more activated trying to memorize the name of the streets and routes. Memories of some birds are different. During the season they must store seeds and food in different places to retrieve later. They can memorize up to an estimated 10,000 different places where they have stored their food for off season use. Their brain cells get deactivated, even make a few new neurons during off season…and there they go again, year after year.

To summarize, Buzz's brain and memory was like that of a bird who drove a taxi on the streets of New York and London combined. Buzz got married to his high school sweetheart, Mary, at her age of 25. Let's listen in as they talk.

"Let's go somewhere hun. We have been working so hard," Buzz said.

"Where do you want to go honey?" Mary asked.

"Anywhere….let's just get in the car and go. We will just go randomly and let our car take us wherever it wants. I really don't care. Who said we have to decide…we will let our car and the wavy roads decide where we will end up. Isn't that the case in our lives anyway? Randomly the world moving us around as we are controlled by so many events…most of them not under our control? Let's suppress our so called Freewill, if we have any, and go anywhere without our will controlling it," Buzz told Mary.

"Ok honey, let's go. Let me get ready," Mary says excitedly.

"I am ready. Let's just take some water and cold cuts in case our getaway ride takes us a little longer," Buzz said.

Buzz and Mary got on the road. They just had a goal in mind to get away from their busy life…at least for a few hours and go to a creek somewhere in the woods north of the town.

"Make a swift turn hun…let's get some gas. The next gas station is miles away and we are almost out," Mary told Buzz, who was driving Mary's SUV.

After getting gas Buzz and Mary reached the destination. They were enjoying their time by the bank of a creek. This was a familiar creek as they had come here a few times. They had this place in mind and here they are. The sound of the river was so relaxing for them both.

"Mary, get some woods gathered and let's start a fire by the creek. It is so peaceful here. It was just a few weeks ago that I came back from the Space Station orbiting the Earth doing some scientific research. Is this the same Earth? God I can't believe that I am back here on terra firma again. From the distance it looks and feels so different," Buzz told Mary.

"Honey, it is so good to feel you and to touch you sitting next to me. Your warmth gives me such a nice feeling. By the way…you used the word God? I can't believe that you uttered that word after writing so many scientific articles against God," Mary stated.

"My mistake, it is just that when you see the Earth way out there…just a blue beautiful marble…it makes you wonder if there was another force who made this planet. Ok…how about calling god GODIA? God If Any," Buzz asked.

"What a wonderful idea…a nicer name for God. At least that will finally create some kind of peace and harmony between the atheists and God lovers, and maybe between many nations," Mary replied.

"Yeah, I know they have been at each other's throat for centuries," Buzz commented.

"Hey Mary, why do they call our planet a blue planet? With so much killings built into its biological fabric it really should be called a red planet, don't you think? I mean…when you look at some of these documentaries about animals on television, the only thing you see is this animal tricking the others to eat them. They go after the most vulnerable ones…normally the little newly born, the weaker ones. I sometimes scream and do not want the little ones to be torn apart. You have heard me scream 'go, go get away' but then ugh, the last breath. They know they need to go for the throat for a quick kill. Who taught them that anyway?" Buzz asked, with heaviness. "I guess their parents, who else?" Buzz told Mary.

"You are right hun, it is killings all over in the animal kingdom, but we are no different than the most savage ones anyway. At least when animals are not hungry they don't go for another kill…but look at some humans…they have so much ego for power," Mary said.

"You are right, but some animals have ego as well…especially monkeys. Maybe because they are the closest to us. They fight as well for power and territory, and of course for sex. It is the problem with our creation. I can't even call it a problem…that is just the way the animated ones are, assembled this way by nature," Buzz said.

"Buzz do you believe in Freewill or you think we are controlled by a deity, or God of religion?" Mary asked.

"Well, that is the hardest question. You have to have a deeper discussion about what is meant by free. The soul, if any…the forces in the physical world…the quantum fields and what is meant by the concept of will. We only know about five percent of what the Universe consists of, so how can you have a definite answer to the Freewill question. How about when a person controls another? Does the person lose his freewill?" Buzz asked.

"Hun did I tell you that when you were in the Space Station there was a murder in town? It is becoming a murder mystery. They are searching for the killer. You probably were not following the news way up there, my space man," Mary tells him.

"Yeah we were so occupied with many different science projects and space walks. I went for a spacewalk and went ten miles away from the Space Station," Buzz said.

"Ten miles? Were you not scared? And why ten miles? What were you doing ten miles away?" Mary asked.

"Well I can't tell you…it is just one of those secrets. Maybe I was target practicing down here. I can only tell you that I was testing how a small device on earth could become activated by sending a sine-wave pulse from the device I had with me. But I can tell you that nobody else knows about what went through my mind…just me and my god…sorry my GODIA. To be honest with you, I was a little bit scared. What if something goes wrong? Will I see my Mary again? But I was so motivated and with so many tests and scientific minds behind these space walks, I knew nothing would go wrong. I am an astronaut, a chemist and a neuroscientist. I was assuring myself that I can control my neurotransmitters that can cause phobia," Buzz explained.

"Neurotransmitters? What is that Hun?" Mary asked.

"Oh dear, I will tell you all about them later. It takes some time to go into the detail. It is a huge subject. We are controlled by them. So who killed who honey?" Buzz asked.

"The killer is on the loose, but the lady who was murdered was the double person for the head of the World Bank," Mary explains.

"Why her?" Buzz asked.

"They don't know yet, but they think that maybe the head of the World Bank was the target. Apparently her billionaire friends have put up ten million dollars to find the killer. The head of the World Bank says she is so devastated and distressed that her double, who had become a good friend of hers, was killed," Mary replied.

"Can you imagine Mary being in her shoes?" Buzz asked.

"I know, it must so hard to see a friend killed…especially your double who was trying to save your own life. The double, named Anna or something has four children…two in college and two teenagers," Mary replied.

"Ugh, oh my god, oh my god," Buzz screamed pulling his leg into his stomach on a rapid reflex move.

"What happened honey?" Mary screamed back.

"Ugh, I think something bit me…something bad…it hurts so bad. It's on my ankle," Buzz says as he pointed down towards his feet.

"Take your shoes and socks off. There you go, you are a strong man," Mary reassured him.

"It feels like it is a strong venom of some kind…it is affecting my nerves," Buzz explained.

"Was it a mosquito or a bee?" Mary asked.

"Are you kidding me? I told you it is so painful. Oh, there it went… it was a snake," Buzz exclaimed with panic in his voice.

"Ok hun, there it went, yup. It had some yellow spots all over," Mary said pointing to the fleeing snake.

"Get in the car Mary. Let's go…take some ashes from the burned wood. I can't drive with this awful pain, so you drive. And before we go put some of the ashes and ice on the bite spot for me. Just rub it in. It is bleeding from the bite site. This pain is killing me…..it is spreading," Buzz says, as they make their way to the car.

"Honey I can't drive on the highways…you know that. And wait a second…let me put the closest hospital in my GPS," Mary said.

"I know dear but do your best to go through the highways. Rush it, that will be our only chance to get to a hospital before I die. It's our only chance," Buzz told Mary, being severely in pain.

"Are you ok my Buzzy Buzz?" Mary asked.

"Not really. I feel the venom is spreading. It is a shooting pain…I even feel numbness around my lips. Ugh this pain. Oh God I don't want to die, I want to live," Buzz said, feeling more pain spreading. Buzz forgot all about Godia and is now calling on "God" to help. He was in danger of dying so that is probably why. He wanted to feel closer to a creator of some kind.

"Please call 911, I am passing out…may have a seizure. Get in the car and go. I will be in the back seat…more leg room there. Go fast. Don't worry about the police," Buzz urged.

"Ok I am dialing 911. Get in the car," Mary replied trying to calm Buzz.

Buzz was laying down on the back seat, but he was trying to keep the bite site below the heart.

"This is 911, what is your emergency?" The operator asked

"Yes please, please, my husband just passed…I mean passed out. He got a bite from a rattle snake by the river. We saw the rattle snake…it had yellow spots all over the body," Mary explained.

"Ma'am, calm down, is he breathing and where are you heading to? We know exactly where you are, so don't try to tell me about your location. Is he breathing I asked, and please answer my question," the operator pressed.

"Yes, to the best I can tell he is," Mary replied.

"Where are you heading to and where is your husband?" asked the operator.

"I am driving on a highway going toward the closest hospital…I have put the address in my GPS," Mary said.

"Stop driving ma'am. The next hospital is an hour away from where you are. Is he in the back seat?" The operator asked but didn't give room for a response. "I have already notified the police to come and close the highways. They will have a medical helicopter to come and get you. Just be calm. Stay on the phone with me until they come. Park on the extreme right side of the highway and stay in the car…it is safer,"

"Ok I will ma'am…thank you so much for helping us," Mary squeaked.

"You are welcome ma'am, just let me know when they have arrived. They should be there by now…they are amazingly fast," the operator finished as Mary heard the helicopter overhead.

"They are here ma'am. Are they going to transport him to the hospital?" Mary asked.

"Yes ma'am. Let them be in charge and don't interfere…they know their job very well. You can go now, goodbye and everything will be fine. You are in good hands," The operator reassured her.

"Goodbye ma'am, and God bless you. Thank you again," Mary said.

The helicopter brought Buzz and Mary to the Emergency section of the hospital where priorities change constantly, but the doctors already knew that he may die any second and gave him priority over the other patients. He was given an anti-venom shot especially made for rattle snake venom.

So, let's go to the emergency section of the hospital where Buzz and Mary were taken and see what is going on. The ER doctor told the nurse in a hurried way for him to get an anti-venom shot.

"Ok doc, done," The nurse said.

"And give him a Fosphenytoin shot to reduce the chance of a seizure, ok?" the doctor told the nurse.

"Ok doc…will give him in a second," the nurse said before giving him the shot.

It did help the doctors when Mary told the operator that the snake had yellow spots on the body. Anti-venom, or anti-venom immunoglobulin, is made from antibodies which is used to treat certain venomous bites and stings. It is used only if there is much high risk of toxicity.

Now let us leave the hospital and do another Quantum Jump and go to the White House and listen in as the Directors of the FBI and CIA are meeting with the President at the Oval Office.

"Mr. President, we have had a lot of chatters and we don't like them. The chatters mostly surround Chima, but with some apparent coordination with their allies, Rubbas," the head of the CIA told the President.

"Well if that is the case let's call the Chairman of the Joint Chiefs of Staff to the meeting," the President said. So, the meeting adjourned and started back again in an hour.

The Director of CIA told the President that Rubbas and Chima's cooperation has elevated to an extremely dangerous degree in that the chatters are now not between their agents, but between their satellites. They are dangerously and constantly repositioning their geostationary satellites. The chatters that they picked up indicated that any attack can come from space and it may not just be a military attack. Could it be chemical? Could it be biological?

Since the military's concerns included medical and biological attacks, they recommended that they invite the head of the CDC and a medical team of bio experts to attend the daily meetings, as well and to see if they can unravel what this may mean in biological terms.

They tell the President that the chatters included terms such as "Dead Agents" and "The Power of Agency" with a character looking like a small inverted V.

"We have engaged our military, CDC, CIA and FBI agents to find out what this code may denote," The Military Chief of Staff said.

The head of the Space Force told the President that they know that Chima and Rubbas have been substantially increasing the number of satellites launched and put into their intended orbits in the right longitude positions. The problem is that they have been able to have them continually repositioned. He continues to tell the President that the thrusters have been firing along the direction and against the direction of the orbit with the correct Delta V. The Artificial Intelligence between the satellites are perfectly accurate and much in line with the uneven gravitational field of the earth, the pull the moon, and the Sun. Very sophisticated.

"We are more concerned about constant changes of their one thousand satellites orbital planes and not their speed...which requires much more propellant than just altitude change. These are not spy satellites but special operational maneuverable satellites. Some of them can grab other satellites or even shoot strong lasers to incapacitate them, causing malfunction. The chatters between satellites have an unusual amount of medical related verbiage, which is seen for the first time. A team from the CDC was assembled immediately and has become a part of our military briefing at the highest level," the military Chief concluded.

Let's leave this presidential briefing meeting now and jump back to our story line with Buzz and Mary after they leave the hospital.

"Hey Buzz, you survived the rattle snake venom. Not everyone can. You were really lucky," Mary told Buzz.

"Oh yeah, lucky that I had you with me and some good emergency room doctors around. The best medical system in the world. I am not saying it cannot be improved, but better than these socialist systems, provided you have money of course…but that is a much larger debate hun," Buzz said talking so proudly about our healthcare system.

Now let us do another Quantum Jump and go to the District Attorney's office and see what is happening over there. We are now at the DA office building.

The sound of squeaking shoes of the experienced District Attorney, Justice Kennedy, on the concrete corridor was so penetrating as he walked from wall to wall of the corridors talking to his deputies. His parents, an African American couple, had given him the first name Justice…maybe they had not seen much justice in their lifetime.

"God damn it. We have tried and tried, and so far no motives and no clues as to who has killed this woman. This is such a strange case. How could we not have any good lead yet?" Justice asked his assistants.

"We do have the blood and some skin tissues found at the scene. They are getting the result of the DNA test to match it against our vast DNA database. We have to find out if they were the victim's or the killer's blood and skin first," His assistant said.

"We have done the search of the area. Our Federal and State agents have contacted all local gas stations, businesses, and have reviewed all their recordings. We have reviewed many of their videos in detail to see if we can establish any pattern for any vehicle or a person moving around. Damn it, no videos that can help us, at least not yet," Justice said.

"We have reviewed everything for the past few days. It was a very time consuming and expensive process. I have heard that we have a couple of big shot donors who have promised to cover some of our expenses. You know we are over our budget for the year. We have no choice but to find this god damn killer one way or another. He won't get away from justice. This Justice…I will find him," Mr. Kennedy says, with confidence.

A few days passed.

"We got the DNA result and we do have a match but a disappointing one and extremely strange result. The blood and the skin matches a person that for sure had not been there….could not have possibly been at the crime scene…we know that for a fact. There has to be an error. Either the blood test is wrong, or our DNA database is wrong," The DA concludes.

"This cannot be true, and we don't want to make an ass out of ourselves by making any announcements to the public and be so wrong. I don't know if we need to contact this man's employer and ask for help or what?" The assistant told Justice Kennedy.

"So, what can we do? Let's get our State agents working on this case to go over their analysis and our options. We need to hold a couple of hours of brainstorming. This cannot be true. How could someone orbiting the Earth be in two places? No way, damn it. This is not quantum mechanics. How can we tell that a well-known astronaut was in two locations at the same time? He was doing a spacewalk orbiting the Earth and killed an innocent person in a remote park? He must have been framed. Should we call him in and ask him some questions?" The assistant asked the DA, Justice Kennedy.

"No way…at least not for now. We cannot tell him that we will charge him for a murder when he was way up there…we can't. But the blood tests are so accurate, as strange as it is. We should re-examine our DNA pool just to make sure that by any remote chance our DNA data pool has not been compromised. Let's do a retest of the blood…and the skin as well," the DA said.

"Of course, I will get those done sir," The assistant replied.

The results of the blood and skin retest came back.

"Oh, my goodness how could this be true? The result of the retest matches with Buzz Armstrong's. We have to find out where he lives and question him without notifying him first or giving any clue to anyone. Let's keep this in our close circle," Mr. Kennedy said.

"What a similarity his name has with the late Neil Armstrong and Buzz Aldrin…this is Buzz Armstrong," His assistant remarked.

Justice Kennedy's office did more research and tested the blood for the third time. Low and behold it matched the blood of our Buzz! But how? How in the world could this be possible? He has to have been framed.

"Well let's go ahead and call him in," Justice Kennedy decided.

"Should we ask this astronaut to give us a new blood sample or should we just ask him to come in and answer a few basic questions?" DA's assistant wondered aloud.

"Damn it, what questions can we ask him? He will laugh at us if we even give him any clue as to why we want his sample, but do we have any other choice? As a minimum we need to find out if he has been a blood donor in the recent past…or if he has had any recent surgeries. We can get some information about his friends, if he thinks he has been framed by someone. We need to find out if he has had any adversaries or competitors who possibly framed him," The DA said.

"Are you suggesting that potentially another astronaut got mad and framed Mr. Armstrong?" Justice's assistant asked, with curiosity.

"No, not quite…but as you know we have seen many cases that the urge to win a god damn piece of gold had become the driving factor in another person's mind, pushing her to frame another person or causing physical harm. Damn it, we know gold is better than silver, but framing someone to get a piece of that gold shit? Oh Lord help us…this is damn crazy," Justice said as his mind reeled, trying to uncover the truth. "Yeah I have seen a good many cases when the person was framed. We will arrange a brainstorming session and do what it takes. My name is Justice…and justice will prevail," The DA said with confidence, making himself loud and clear.

"Let's go ahead and call him in. We need to let him know about the case and of course read him his Miranda rights, just in case…but we have to take the case to a Grand Jury before charging him. We probably don't need to do that…at least not yet. This is just to tell him about the blood test and ask for help. I wonder if he'll cooperate?" The assistant bantered.

So, they call Buzz Armstrong at NASA. The operator answers the phone in a friendly voice. "Good morning, this is NASA, how may I direct your call?"

"Hello ma'am, this is Justice Kennedy, State attorney for the Orlando District,"

"Good morning Mr. Kennedy, how may I direct your call, sir?" The operator asked again.

"Yes, I would like to talk to astronaut Buzz Armstrong," Mr. Kennedy answered.

The operator answered after a pause saying, "Let me see if I can get him on the phone for you sir,"

"Thank you ma'am," Mr. Kennedy answered, in a friendlier voice to ease her mind.

He was put on hold briefly and then she came back on the line. "I am so sorry, but his office states that he is in an extremely important meeting and cannot take a call right now. Can I have him call you back Mr. Kennedy?"

"Yes of course, I understand. Just let him know that I called, I will call him back tomorrow…or he can call me. I thank you ma'am, have a good day," Justice said before he left his name and number, leaving out telling her why he had called.

Buzz goes home and tells Mary that he got a call from the District Attorney.

"I am wondering why in the world the DA had called me?" Buzz said to Mary.

Mary becomes extremely nervous and shaking, as if she knew of some reasons for him to get a call. Mary asks Buzz if they gave any clues as to why he had called, but Buzz doesn't have any other information. The next day Justice Kennedy reaches Buzz Armstrong and asks him to come to his office. They meet that same day.

"Good Afternoon, Mr. Armstrong…how are you sir? I am Justice Kennedy and here is my assistant, Mr. John Knight," Mr. Kennedy said as they all greeted each other.

"Can you tell me why I am here and how I may be able of any help to you?" Buzz asked, a bit anxious.

"Well, the reason we called you is to ask for your assistance in solving a murder case. A lady was murdered, and we are trying to get some clues as to who may have committed this heinous murder," Justice explained, careful not to say too much.

"Is the name Anna…something by any chance," Buzz asked.

Justice Kennedy's eyes widened, but he tried to hide his wonder. "Yes, that's right…Anna Rodriguez. How did you know about that Mr. Armstrong?"

"Well, it looks like it's all over the news. That, and my wife told me that when I was doing research in the Space Station a lady by that name was murdered," He explained casually.

"Oh ok, yes. It is good that you have also heard about the case," the DA answered.

"But why…and how do you think I can be of any help to you Mr. Kennedy?" Buzz wondered aloud.

"Well, that is the big mystery and there is a good reason why we have asked you to come in," Mr. Kennedy said carefully.

"Oh no problem, I will do my absolute best," Buzz said, staying calm.

"Normally when we ask people to come in and answer questions…especially in a murder case, we take the case to the Grand Jury and charge the person and read him or her their Miranda Rights, or ask him to bring his or her attorney," the DA began to explain.

"You don't need to read me that, Sir. There is no case in the world that is related to me that needs Miranda Warning to be read...so don't be concerned...I waive my rights for that," Buzz jumped in with interruption.

"Well, just to let you know...you can stop us at any moment or have an attorney present...or just refuse to give an answer to any of our questions... you can take the fifth you know," Mr. Kennedy says, in a dutiful voice.

"Oh no...no need for that," Buzz said with a chuckle. "I won't take the first, the second, the third, the fourth or the fifth. Is that enough or should I carry on?" Buzz made fun and light of the questioning and continued. "Let's get on with the case and I will do my best to give you any information possible...not that I have any information or clues," Buzz assured him.

"Well, we found some blood and skin at the murder scene and have done the DNA test and have matched the result with our master DNA database," Justice begins to explain.

"Ok great, I know the government database is quite big and secure and well managed," Buzz said, with confidence, wanting to show his support to the government he worked for.

"Yes sir, it is," Justice agreed. "And the surprising thing is that the test result matches *your* DNA,"

Buzz started laughing, but controlled himself as Justice glared at him, unamused.

"Oh great...oh yeah I know...I had a big gun at the Space Station and shot the lady from way up there. Ha! Or maybe I used a radar to activate a laser gun or an electronic knife or something, killing the lady as she was walking in the woods," Buzz told the DA, somewhat mockingly.

"Seriously we are puzzled because we know you were orbiting the Earth when she was murdered. But your blood was found at the scene, and that is why we have asked you to come in and help us. We don't have any clues as to why, but we are still trying to put the strange pieces of the puzzle together. We believe you are the key in solving this mystery," Mr. Kennedy told Buzz.

"Ok. I will do my best, but you still have not told me how I can be of any help," Buzz said, with curiosity.

"For one thing Mr. Armstrong, do you have any reason to believe that someone may have framed you by putting your blood and skin at the scene of the crime? Have you donated any blood…or have you gone to any of these local medical outfits for possible injury?" Justice Kennedy asked, trying to get to the meat of the questions.

"Well I always give blood…and the last one I gave was about a few months ago. Yes I did recently cut my hand…but unfortunately we did not go to any of NASA's special clinics for treatment. We are not allowed to go to unknown places," Buzz replied.

"If you don't mind, will you tell us where you went to give blood?" Mr. Kennedy asked, pulling out his notepad.

"Of course not…it was a local Mosque on Main Street, around the corner here," Buzz replied, gesturing with his hand.

Justice made a mental note to contact them to see if there was any additional information they could give him and then asked, "Was it their special blood donation center, or was it at the Mosque itself?"

"No, it was a blood collection drive right in the Mosque…you know, just like some Churches do with Red Cross with blood drives," Buzz explained, puzzled.

"Oh ok, no problem. Is there anything else you can tell us Mr. Armstrong? And can we talk to your wife as well?" The DA asked, peering at Buzz and trying to understand him further.

"Nothing more that will help you…but how could my wife be of any help to you?" Buzz questioned.

"Well we don't know exactly, but since she is the closest to you on a daily basis we may find out if you have had any adversaries that may have had an intention to frame you…because we know one thing…the blood and skin found at the murder scene matches yours. That is the only clue we have so far and so we have no choice but to follow it," Mr. Kennedy explained.

"Um…., well of course, you can call her and ask her to come in…or you can come visit her at our house," Replied Buzz eagerly.

"We will probably just come to your house…if you don't mind. This way we can also look at the neighborhood to possibly get some other clues," The DA explained casually.

"Ok please do so and she will have some good, freshly brewed coffee ready for you if you'd like" Added Buzz.

"Sure. One last question…and please don't be offended. Can you tell us if you have had any marital problems…especially any fresh arguments in the last few months?" The DA prodded carefully.

"Oh goodness gracious…you are not trying to blame my wife for framing me, are you? Oh no…no, no way that could have been the case. No way sir," Buzz said with a bit of anger.

"No I'm not blaming anyone…not at all. It's just always good to know about any marital problems…and please don't take it personally. These are just routine questions," Mr. Kennedy told him, with ease.

"Of course, I am ok being asked personal questions. And now that you have asked me I have to give you an honest answer," Buzz declared and then paused. "We have had some marital problems. I had been thinking about separation, but she is totally against it. You know…when you travel so much… and for so long sometimes…it is best to be single…you know…not fair to the wife," Buzz added.

They talked about the case for another fifteen minutes and wrapped up their discussion. As Buzz is leaving their office and driving home, he goes into deep thinking.

After another brainstorming session held between the attorneys at the DA office Justice becomes curious and wants to talk to Buzz's wife, so they call Mary.

"Good morning, Mrs. Armstrong. This is Justice Kennedy. I am sure Mr. Armstrong has told you about us and the problem we have at hand," He starts with a kind and friendly tone.

"Good morning sir. Yes, he did talk to me very briefly about the case, and he mentioned that you may want to talk to me," Mary replied, a little quiet.

"Yes, and that is great that you are somewhat familiar with our case. In fact, it's an exceedingly difficult case. We were wondering if we can ask you to help us solve this murder mystery?" Justice asked.

"Yes sir, but…how can I be of any help to you though?" Mary answered, unsettled.

"Well, we don't know, but we can come to your house and see you, and of course we prefer that Mr. Armstrong not to be present when we meet you," Mr. Kennedy explained carefully.

"Of course, I don't see any problem with the meeting, but why should my husband not be with me? He is the closest person to me, you know," Mary responded with seriousness.

"Well that is our preference, but we will leave it up to you, of course. And if you prefer you can have an attorney present too," The DA told Mary, who all of a sudden becomes nervous being told that she could have an attorney present.

The DA office makes the arrangements for the meeting. Justice Kennedy and his assistants meet Mrs. Armstrong in her house, and she had asked Buzz not to be present. When Buzz was told that he should not be in the meting he did not mind, but Mrs. Armstrong did not like that idea at all and became a bit nervous and agitated.

"Well, you are the closest person to me... This is ridiculous...I am outraged! Why wouldn't they want you to be here?" Mary asks loudly.

"I don't know...but why should we even care?...we haven't done anything wrong, have we? He will ask a few questions and you will answer them truthfully and that is all. Then they will go their way and leave us alone unless you...,"

Buzz hadn't finished his sentence as Mary interrupted with a yell and said, "Don't you dare say what you were going to say!"

"Honey, I was only going to say that if you want, I can cancel the appointment and have them meet with our attorney and not you," Buzz responded quickly, as he tried to cool her down.

"Well you are my husband. What if they ask me a question and I give them a wrong answer?! You know I am not an attorney, and to be honest with you I do prefer to have our attorney present anyway," Mary told Buzz as she seemed to become more puzzled by the situation.

"Ok dear, we will have our attorney present. I know it will be a waste of money...and you know how much they charge an hour. Anyway...there is no way in the world that they would consider me or you as a potential suspect," Buzz said firmly.

"I know honey, but please arrange for him to be here," Mary said, trying to calm herself.

So, the day came when DA Justice Kennedy meets Mrs. Armstrong with their attorney, Abel Dershowitz, present with her. Buzz was not present at the meeting. He had gone to one of the local coffee shops to get out of the house and get a cup of coffee. After they go through introducing themselves the DA starts his questioning.

"Mrs. Armstrong, you don't know how much we appreciate your assistance and cooperation in this matter. Mr. Armstrong may have told you already that your husband's blood and skin have been found at the murder scene of Ms. Anna Rodriguez. We also know that at the time he was away, as a matter of fact way, way up there orbiting the Earth, he told us that recently he donated blood in your local Mosque. So nice of him to do that. Were you aware of that and were you with him that day?" DA Justice asked Mary.

"Yes sir, and I gave blood too. We have been in that Mosque a few times... they are good people. We get invitation to go there once every now and then, not very often though. They have our email address in their database," Mary answered, trying to stay settled.

"Have they been friendly with you and Mr. Armstrong? What I mean is that have you or Mr. Armstrong had any arguments with their leaders or members at any time?" The DA asked.

"Yes sir, as a matter of fact my husband's feeling about God is so different from theirs and he had argued with them in a few very heated arguments. Truthfully, he loves arguing and debating people about God," Mary stated.

"Any names over there?" asked Justice.

"Yes sir, I will email you their contact information," Mary said, making a mental note to take care of that as soon as the meeting was finished.

"Thanks, and let me ask you another question," started the DA. "Has Mr. Armstrong had any injury in the recent past at home requiring any medication or stitches?"

"Yes sir, he cut his hand cutting some cucumbers making salad, it was pretty bad, some skin came off and it was bleeding very badly. He wanted to go to the local clinic but then he said he was not allowed to, so I cleaned the extra skin off and cleaned the area and...uh," she stopped suddenly as Mrs. Armstrong's attorney steps in and holds her hand, pinching and squeezing a bit in trying to give her a clue that she is going too far with her explanation to silently tell her to stop answering any further questions. The attorney very cordially and softly asks the DA and his associates to leave for now until he talks to Mary.

"Yes sir," The DA tells her attorney, with curiosity. "We understand that and believe me we are not trying to connect the dots that will point to you, Mrs. Armstrong, but as you know when we have to unravel a murder mystery case and to do that, we have to turn any and all possible stones and follow any clues we can find," The DA told Mary and her attorney.

"Yes sir, we know that, and we appreciate your effort, but you gave me a chill by trying to bring Mrs. Armstrong into this, and frankly I just did not like your aggressive style of questioning her. You know, not having been around any FBI agent or any prosecutor Mrs. Armstrong appeared and actually became nervous, even when she was telling you the truth, so please don't take her nervousness as a clue in solving your murder mystery case," The attorney said looking concerned.

"Oh no, not at all sir, we appreciate that you are trying to defend your client and you believe that she had nothing to do with this murder, but you know the problem is that in our daily jobs our agents deal with so many lies, and so they have no choice but to ask these questions. They cannot overrule any possibility that the person may be lying, not that Mrs. Armstrong is, however we thank you both very much for at least now we have some clues as to where the blood and especially the skin may have come from and we will be in touch again," The DA said, looking very happy as if they got their person. After all, who else has had Mr. Armstrong's skin and blood other than Mary Armstrong?

The DA held another brainstorming session with his assistants and now they have more clues. They know that the wife had some skin tissue and blood from him, they saw a possibility of a revengeful act stemming from the fact that Buzz wants to divorce her.

The DA, his deputies, and the prosecutor talk more about whether they should ask her to come in with her attorney for further questioning, or if they should go to a Grand Jury now or wait? They know that without him being on Earth at the time of the murder the possibility of having his blood, and especially his skin at the scene of the murder almost impossible, so they conclude that it had definitely been planted at the murder scene. But by Mary his beloved wife?

Next, they turn their attention to the whereabouts of Mrs. Armstrong's car on that specific day and they found that her car was nearly at the murder scene on that date, in the city and that area, just a mile from the murder scene. Being an experienced DA, Justice followed all the rules and went through the court system to legally get corroborating information, the whereabouts of her cell phone, among other pieces of information.

"Well her car was a mile away from the actual murder scene, but maybe she walked, or possibly she could have hired another person to do the murder and gave the blood and skin tissue to be planted by the hired killer. She appeared too weak to have done that herself, as I did not see in her the ability to commit such a murder and get away with it," The DA told his assistants.

"Well let's look at other surveillance cameras. We also need to examine her telephone records and we have to get a court order to do that," The assistant reminded.

Well the DA analyzed her telephone records. It showed many calls to some people on that day and in that area. The DA takes further action and investigates those persons' whereabouts on that day.

The District Attorney and his assistant interview Mrs. Armstrong and her attorney again asking many other questions about their marriage.

After obtaining other records and not having any other information or clues the best clue the DA had was pointing to Mrs. Armstrong, so they finally decided to go to a Grand Jury and ask for her to be charged with the murder of Anna Rodriguez. The only thing they don't have is the murder weapon but there have been many cases in the past that the person got convicted without the murder weapon found. In those cases, they got conviction only based on circumstantial evidence, much more difficult to convict, but they have no other suspect but Mary.

"Mrs. Armstrong is the only person that we know who had his skin and blood," the DA tells the Jurors and continues, "we also found out that her car and her phone were in the area very close to where the murder happened on that day. She has had some marital problems as well and therefore we believe she is the one who has murdered this poor woman and somehow framed Mr. Armstrong," The DA finished telling the Grand Jury.

"Did you, as a prosecutor ask her if her car and or her cell phone were stolen or whether she loaned it to another person for a day or two? Possibly a friend of theirs needed a car, or some of their friends came from out of town and needed transportation?" One of the Jurors asked.

"We should have, I know we will during the trial," The DA said, who was a bit angry that they had not asked her those questions.

"But sir, you are asking us to charge this lady for a murder without properly doing your job and she does not have her attorney here. What is this nonsense?" Another Juror asked with an angry voice.

"You told us that he gave blood at the local mosque and that they had a bit of disagreement with them," "did you follow up sir to see if the Mosque leader or any of their members were involved and had planted the blood at the murder scene?" One more Juror asked.

"Good question sir. We did not, because they did not have his skin and it was not probable that there was any collusion between Mrs. Armstrong and the mosque," The DA replied with confidence.

"Well, you are saying probably this and probably that, do you really expect us to believe that this lady killed someone with this bunch of probable nonsense you are giving us? Probably you should be removed from this case. Probably you should be fired by doing such a lousy job," Another angry Juror said, being terribly upset. The DA just ignored the comment.

Well, after presenting a one-sided case, which is normal, the Grand Jury based on these facts and reviewing other records, gave the District Attorney what he had asked for: a premeditated murder charge against Mrs. Armstrong.

They called Mrs. Armstrong and gave her the news and asked her to turn herself in. She is devastated, but she had no other choice but to turn herself in after talking to her attorney who is also extremely upset. Buzz is outraged. The news gets spread all over the country. All astronauts, the NASA administrators feel upset about the news and they cannot believe that Mary has been charged. They reassure Buzz that if he needed their help, they are there for him and his family.

Buzz gets a telephone call not just from the President of the United States but the President of Chima to show support and sympathy. But why Chima? Why is Chima's President so concerned about Buzz's wife being charged? Strange. Has she been in contact with any Chimese agents? We should not weave any conspiracy with Chima into this. Not yet.

With the help of her attorney and Buzz, they persuade the presiding Judge and Mary gets bailed out with some limitations. A week passes and everyone is puzzled and dazed. Mary and Buzz argue about the case. At some point their discussion gets heated. As Mr. and Mrs. Armstrong are having a discussion with their attorney one of their old friends unexpectedly knocks on their door to come and see them. They place their argument on hold, as they had not seen him for a long time.

Ding Dong. Mary peeks through the little viewing hole, so surprised to see an old friend at the door waiting. She opens the door.

"Come on in Fred, how are you dear? Goodness gracious, we haven't seen you for almost a year! Where have you been hiding?" Give me a hug," Mary excitedly greets him.

"I know, I missed you guys so much, I was just passing by and said to myself, let me just pop in. Sorry I didn't call you before I came... hey Buzz how are you man?" Fred asked with happy relief that the door was answered.

After greeting and hugging with their old friend they introduce their attorney to him. They nod to one another and settle in.

"I know I had not seen Mary for about a year or so, but I was so happy that I saw Buzz last week," Fred said.

"Last week?" Buzz asked amazed, after very quickly turning his head to look at Fred giving him a short but sharp look. He asks Fred with wonder as to what Fred was talking about. Mary becomes curious and focuses her attention on the two old friends.

"My god I have not seen you Fred for a long time...what are you talking about?" Asked Buzz"

"Are you drunk, my friend?! We met at the Starbucks on Johnson Ferry Road... was it last Saturday or Sunday, I'm not sure," Fred replied, so sure.

"Maybe you *are* drunk Fred. Have you been smoking something? I have not been to that Starbucks for a couple of years...I know that for sure," Buzz said with an irritated voice.

Mary jumps into the discussion, very curious. Hahaha, what in the world are you guys talking about?" Buzz did you go to that coffee shop honey? Tell me. It is ok if you met someone that you do not want me to know. Any of those NASA secret meetings?"

Now Mary is thinking that possibly Buzz was meeting a girlfriend. After all, they are having marital problems, but who knows?

"Oh my god what have I said to cause problems here....stupid me, just shut up," Fred says, talking to himself.

"Oh no, I swear I have not been there for a couple of years," Buzz answered looking to Fred, as if he wants him to change the story. "Fred are you sure it was me?" "there are a couple of Starbucks close to our house. I know I am not that forgetful," Buzz asked again.

"I know it was you. We had a cup of coffee and we even did a selfie together; don't you remember?" Fred asked.

"No, I don't remember," Buzz said with a bit of anger.

Mary storms out to bring coffee and Fred talks with Buzz in a whispery way.

"Hey Buzz, you were talking to that beautiful girl when I saw you and when I came to you to say hello you acted a bit like you didn't even know me. I probably should not have interrupted your warm discussion with her. The lady was so nice to ask me to sit with you guys and we talked for a couple of minutes. I thought you were embarrassed that I saw you with the girl and that is why you acted so cold towards me. I had to rush out to go to an appointment, but we did a selfie together, remember? You acted very strange...talking to the girl about God," Fred told Buzz.

Mary overhears the conversation and comes in and asks to see the selfie. The three of them gather around Fred's phone and look at the picture. Mary becomes curious to see who the girl was, and if she was in the picture or somewhere in the coffee shop. Their attorney is curious, as well but he is just watching, wondering what is going on here.

"Well, that is you Buzz!" Mary says and angrily walks away.

"Yeah that is me, but I know I was not there....and look, I have never ever had a black shirt like that...isn't that true Mary? Mary where are you sweetheart? Come look at the picture again," Buzz calls after Mary.

Buzz finds her face down on their bed crying.

"For goodness sake, what is this, why are you crying honey?" Buzz asks.

He is holding Mary's hand and giving her a kiss on the back of her neck trying to assure her that he had not been in that Starbucks.

Fred stays seated, telling himself "gosh, have I caused a major problem here?" "I have done many stupid things in life, but this tops them all,"

"Come on my love. Let's go look at the picture again," Buzz says as he tries to convince Mary. "Have I ever had a black shirt like that sweetie? The person looks like me, but it is not me...I swear,"

Mary looks at the picture again and confirms, looking a little happier, but still searching for any other woman even in the background of the picture.

"Hey Fred let me see the selfie again, and please forward it to my phone," Mary asked Fred.

"Well this is another mystery, unless you lie Buzz," Mary says flatly.

"Believe me Mary, I am not. Yes that is me in that shirt, but I know I haven't had that kind of shirt ever," Buzz assured Mary.

"I know that. Unless you keep some clothing somewhere else other than in your closet in *this house*," Mary said with skepticism.

"You are not pulling my leg Fred, are you? Have you done a photo shop and changed the picture to tease us?" Buzz asked, hoping for a final positive answer from him.

"No Buzz, why would I do that? I don't even know how to work with Photo Shop, but you know what?" Fred asks.

"What," Both Mary and Buzz asked together.

"I know it was you, but I was surprised to see you with a different tone of voice as you continued talking to the girl. I listened for a couple of minutes, but you were talking good about God with the lady and I know your beliefs about God. The black shirt looked a bit like one of those that preachers wear…not their formal one though. I thought you were a totally different person, inconsistent with the person that I've always known, but then I know it was you…I have no doubt…unless…you don't have an identical twin, do you?" Fred asked Buzz.

"Oh no, I mean I really don't know, but since I was adopted…who knows," Fred answers slowly.

"I bet you that this is the case," Fred says.

Fred acted as if he already knew about the murder case, the news had spread all over and there wasn't hardly anyone who had not heard it. After all Buzz was an incredibly famous person.

Mary rushed into the conversation.

"I hate to say this Buzz, but I bet that you do have an identical twin. Have no doubt. And with my apologies to you, he probably is the one who committed the murder and here I am, poor me, charged with this damn murder," Mary said with a bit of anger but with some hope as well, thinking maybe this will get her conviction reversed.

"Oh, come on Mary, don't get more upset please," Buzz jumped in.

"Please Buzz, don't try to calm me, and don't try to defend your twin brother either. What don't you understand? It's my neck on the line…I am charged with something I have not done," Mary retorted, upset and out of control a bit.

"I am not honey…I am not. I am just asking you not to get upset. We know there is no way that you could have committed this murder. We know that for sure and all we have to do is to prove it," Buzz replied.

"Oh yeah? I know that, but do they? The damn DA has charged me with premeditated murder. I've been crying day and night. What part of this is difficult for you to understand? You are supposed to be a smart astronaut, right?" Mary said raising her voice and continued. "Buzz, we know that you could not have been there. They know that I was the only one who had your blood as well as your skin, as they say. Oh yeah...I had your blood and skin and I went there, killed that woman and left the evidence there to frame you. Is this what you want me to say? Because this is exactly what they think!" Mary said with a red-hot face.

Buzz jumped back in while he had the chance. "Well that is what we need to overcome! It looks confusing even to us as to who in the world could have done this,"

"Oh pleeeeese, don't use those words again. Nothing is confusing to me! Don't you dare...having any suspicion about me. I am so outraged with this whole nonsense you have created Buzz!" Mary says, getting angrier.

"Who me? What have *I* done? I was not even on planet Earth for goodness sake!" Buzz exclaimed and continued. "And I did not have a strong binocular with me to see who the killer was, so what do you want me to say?"

The attorney, having sat in silence long enough jumps in and tells everyone to cool off. "Well we have seen so many cases like this and I assure you both that we will get to the bottom of it. And at the end of the day you will be cleared Mary. So please...calm down...both of you," Their attorney said.

The four of them agree to go to the Starbucks and ask for help. They ask for the surveillance camera videos and after going through the coffee shop's legal obstacles look at them to find the person with a black shirt driving in, parking, and then driving out in a purple Cadillac after being inside for some 30 minutes. They also see Fred's car parked and see Fred in the Starbucks. The video clearly shows the face of Buzz, or someone just like him. They write the license plate number of the car and go directly to the local DMV. There they go through more legal obstacles with the DMV's main office. They finally find the name of person; the person is identified as Innocenti Cristo.

The attorney calls Mr. Cristo and they talk on the phone about the case and asked him if he would be kind enough to go to Buzz and Mary's house on a certain date. The attorney told Innocenti that he knew about Innocenti and his involvement in the church and reminded him that a man of God like him is always there to help others. He told Innocenti that he had no doubt that he would help this family as well to solve this murder mystery. Innocenti agrees to meet them.

At night, Buzz and Mary are in bed talking about the murder case and why Mary was charged. They are both distressed, but should they feel a minor sense of hope now? Not so quickly.

Now you and I must do another Quantum Jump to Innocenti's life, background, and his upbringing. Who is he and how was he raised?

Chapter 5
Innocenti's Upbringing

This lovely man was raised by an exceedingly kind Italian family, Mr. and Mrs. John Cristo. He was named as such because of his innocent looks. He became the pastor of a local church and was involved in many charitable operations. He loved to debate his wife on some philosophical grounds, issues related to his God and the behavior of human beings.

The Cristo family, John and Kristina always wanted to have a child but because John did not have enough strong sperms and Kristina's infertility issues, they could not have a child. Kristina had some hormonal imbalance problems that interfered with her normal ovulation. She never had ectopic surgery and all these problems were ruled out, but at the end of the day and very many loving nights and trials they could not have a child. Still, they had talked about fostering or adopting a child.

We all know that sometimes the forces of the Universe override our "Freewill" to the benefit of another innocent child. In fact, Innocenti was this lucky child. But was he lucky that he was adopted?

Kristina and John used to go to this smooth-running river, always sitting on the grassy soft side of the riverbank, enjoying the day for hours as Kristina was doing her beloved sketching and oil painting. She was selling her paintings at their local church and at various local shows, all for the benefit of the church. This river was an awfully slow running river and many people were coming and sitting there when the weather was perfect. John on the other hand was a free thinker. He was just sitting there watching the natural world thinking about the Universe and why and how we got here. At times he would occupy himself with reading various books on those subjects.

On this beautiful day sitting by this peaceful river listening to the wild birds, John notices a big basket moving on the river surface close to the bank and hears someone saying, "Oh my god, what in the world is in that basket?! It looks like there is a baby in it," A man was pointing to the moving basket on the river, awfully close to the bank.

"Look, look Kristina... what is in that basket coming down?" John asked.

"I don't know, but something is moving in it...maybe someone's cat. Can you get that?" She answers, with curiosity.

"Of course. Let me see...the river is not deep. I can just walk there," John decides.

"Ok honey, go, go quickly. Be careful!" Urges Kristina.

"Oh my God, there *is* a baby in the basket! Looks so innocent. What should we do Kristina?" John asked bringing the basket and showing it to her.

"Well, we need to go to the police station and report this," Kristina said, and then added, "Aren't you happy John? Is God telling us something? And don't they say Finders Keepers?" Kristina carefully said, as happy as one could be.

"Isn't this what we always wanted from God? We wanted a child and here he is, a gift from our loving Lord. Oh he *does* look so innocent. Is it a boy or a girl?" Kristina asked John.

"Let me check. Oh a little boy! Let's call him Innocenti," John said.

They were both so happy talking and already planning for the boy's future. Many other people noticed what was happening and they gathered around the baby, some crying with joy and many were just astonished.

After going through the hell of governmental paperwork Innocenti was formally adopted and raised by this very loving, God fearing family. He was taught to do only good things in life. He studied Theology in a local university and was always committed to helping people in their spiritual formation, from childhood to adulthood. Innocenti was always there to help. All you had to do was just ask. This kind man could not utter the words "no" or "I can't".

Innocenti also taught Theology at a local college and became the pastor of a local church. He was awarded many times as the church membership sky-rocketed and as the church increased its charitable service to the community. He really became a "Jesus-like" person and conformed to the image of Christ helping others. This man continuously challenged himself to think clean, be kind, and follow his God's calling. He was also very culturally focused and always desired to visit the Pope. You may wonder though as to why the Pope, who is sitting on billions of donated cash while the poor suffers, but that is you and I thinking, not Innocenti. His messages were coming from his heart and impacted his followers. He was taken by people's hearts and minds.

Innocenti knew how he was adopted. He did not know about his brother Buzz, even though he was given a clue twice in his life. He thought that even if he did have a brother that he should not interfere with his life. Afterall, maybe his brother's adoptive parents had not told him that he had been adopted and thought maybe he should honor that.

Now another Quantum Jump will take us to Innocenti Cristo and his wife Maria's house.

"Innocenti, are you okay my sweetheart, you handsome man?" Maria asked with genuine care.

"Yes my love, why?" Innocenti answered.

"Oh nothing," Maria replied.

"My dear Maria, please don't give me one of those 'oh nothings' again. Tell me what is on your mind," Innocenti urged.

"Well honey, now that you asked I have to be honest with you. Ever since you had your brain surgery you have been walking and talking a bit…differently. And honestly, you have become a bit more forgetful," Maria said, cautiously.

"Well, if I forget everything else in the world, even if I forget my own name my sweet Maria, I will never ever forget you and your beautiful name …M a r i a," He said with a smile. "And don't worry, my surgeon…who is the best in the world, told me that I did not need to get any MRIs. And if I ever needed an MRI not to go to any other facility but his. I have to trust him since I have not had any problem, no sign of any growth of the old meningioma tumor that I can feel. Thanks to my loving God it was not cancerous. And I have been taking the pills he gave me, and the device shows no major fluctuations whenever I use it," Innocenti reminded her optimistically.

"But Innocenti, you did not have any pain with the big tumor in your brain until that night when you had a seizure. What a night it was for me at the hospital when the result of the X-Ray showed the tumor! Oh it was hell. So please call him," Maria said with an urging love.

"Ok honey, I will call my doctor tomorrow," He promised.

Innocenti as usual was talking about God.

"My sweetheart Maria, you can criticize God as much as you like, yet who but God has given us a chance to live this wonderful life? God has given us a chance to come alive from non-life and see the world. Gathered us from the dust scattered around stars and between. We can now hear the Universe… sense it, taste it, see many of its colors…paint in it, sing in it, listen to Beethoven and enjoy many other wonderful things. But you are right, Mary…I have become a bit forgetful, so I really need to see him," Innocenti said, and continued. "Maria, let me test my memory. Let me see if I remember what we said in our wedding ceremony. This is my solemn vow, I, Innocenti Cristo take you, Maria, to be my wedded wife, I promise to be true to you in good times and in wrong, in sickness and in health, I will love you and honor you all the days of my life. Don't you remember that honey? Shouldn't we apply the same rule to our God, to love him at good times and in bad? I love you Maria, I love you God, I love you Jesus," Innocenti finished quietly.

"Of course dear, as always you are right. That is why you are a church leader. It looks like your memory isn't so bad after all! You remembered all those words and even I couldn't remember those exact words…but now that you are an expert on God issues let me ask you this…and please be honest with me. Why has your god created pain in us? And I know you would say that pain is our body's best defensive system, but couldn't your god have created us without pain and suffering? Even I could have done that if I were the creator," Maria said boldly.

"But my sweet Maria, you claim that now as you are sitting here as God's creature, but if you ended up with that much power you probably would have acted the same way that God did. When you are powerful you don't act like you are powerless," Innocenti said and continued. "Maria, God could have made the world differently, of course he could have. He has Omnipotent power, he is the divine, but he chose not to. And by the way you called me an expert on God's issues…far from the truth. You know all of us, you and I, the so-called Prophets of God, Jesus, Moses, Mohammad, the Pope, and all humans who have come before us and currently live have the same knowledge about God," Innocenti said with confidence.

"And what is it that we or they know about god…what knowledge?" Maria asked.

"Absolutely nothing. I mean absolutely nothing. Not a thing do we know about God, but we assign traits and goodness to God to satisfy ourselves. If God wanted to show himself he would have had an easy time. No beating around the bush…he would have shown up, he would have called all of us on our cell phones, he would have proven himself much, much better," Innocenti said so calmly.

"I cannot believe a man of god is talking like this!" Maria said.

"Well, you told me to be honest with you, and if there is a God I believe there is one. He wants me to be honest with *Him* too. Who knows, maybe he wanted to have fun, or did not want to have a boring world. Maybe he wants us to continue guessing about him, our guesses takes us closer…or sometimes further away from him," Innocenti explained with a gleam in his eyes.

"How do you know that your God is a he? You referred to God as a he as if you know him… after all 'he' has not given us any clues as to 'his' existence, of course 'he' sent us books, the book that you teach, the Bible," Maria told Innocenti.

"Yes, I do teach the Bible, but in all his books he is a self-declared God. If I declare 'I, Innocenti Cristo, I am God' would anyone believe me?" "Heck no!" Innocenti exclaimed.

Maria was amazed and could not believe her ears receiving these words from the man of God she has known and has been living with for so many years. "Are you the same person whom I have lived with for years my man?" Maria asked.

"See honey, first of all my use of the word 'he' is a habit, but I know where you are going with this. I know that this is more of a male dominated world, especially within the church and the Mosques, and that bothers your deep psyche. And it should, I am with you. But all these books are so inconsistent, not just between them but within each. God is a self-declared God with no proof and then in his books he orders us to kill others?" Innocenti asked and stated.

"I can't believe that in your heart that is what you think…I have never seen you talk like that," Maria said asking herself whether something is wrong with Innocenti and his operated brain. Has the tumor come back big time?

"Well, the truth is the truth. It is so hard to find the truth these days. My heart is with Jesus…my brain…sorry my 'half operated brain' tells me a different story," He remarked.

"Did the brain operation change you?" Maria asked.

"Maybe so. I think the brain surgery made me more honest about life. I know our brain changes every second anyway, but who knows, I have noticed changes in my way of thinking and acting, just a bit. You know Maria, have you noticed that nowadays nobody claims that he is a Prophet of God? It is because they know if they claim that right away so many groups will take him to court and challenge him. He won't be able to answer any scientific or common sense questions posed to him in a court of law. I think these talkative attorneys may end up persuading the Judge to have him transferred to a mental institution," Innocenti said.

"Innocenti, billions of people believe in those Prophets. How come, what can you tell them?" Maria questioned.

"Well those old Prophets are not around to be questioned, and also since their claim goes back thousands of years, some people think that they were closer to God. You know, ten thousand years ago there was no such God, but then a spark in only one person's brain created that concept, and it spread like a virus to others...but who knows?" Innocenti answered but reserved some doubts for himself. He did not want to lose his insurance policy in case he finally meets his God.

"I love you honey. Please call your surgeon, okay? It has been sometime since he operated on your brain and took that big tumor out," Reminded Maria.

"Ok, I will call him tomorrow. He has had some problems of his own since his major burn many years ago, especially his face," Innocenti said.

"Yes but, I have been a bit concerned lately. You have started dreaming more often and last night you started screaming and sounded like you were running away from an accident or something like a murder scene. And at some point you sat and cried, and do you know what you said? 'Oh my god, what have I done? I feel so bad, I think she is dead.' Please...just call," Maria pleaded.

"Maria, don't talk like that. It scares me. I will call him tomorrow, okay? You are right, I have noticed that myself. I have felt so aggressive at times, especially when I have a knife in my hand. I will call him," Innocenti reassured her quickly.

"Thank you dear for understanding. All I want is for you to be healthy, both physically and mentally," Maria continued. "Yeah, I have seen certain patterns of aggressive behavior in you, as if it comes and goes. Sometimes you act like you are the kindest person, and then...bang! More meanness in the way you think and act. And I know for a fact that you are the kindest person, a man of god. Thank you for listening to me. You are the best. Have and always will be mine," Maria finished sweetly.

The next day Maria and Innocenti talk about other life issues, his brain and what goes on in someone's brain and the reality of the world. Maria had read some books on quantum physics and wanted to test her own logic against those of Innocenti's, as she knows that the quantum phenomena and common sense don't reconcile and do not go hand in hand.

"I have to ask you this: When you say God is always 'there' for us what do you really mean? Where is that 'there'?" Maria asked carefully.

"I wish I knew Maria, as I told you dear. We know absolutely nothing about God," He replied.

"But the church and god-loving people really believe in a god being '*there*' for them. That is what you always tell them, right? They donate their hard-earned money to you for a god that they think is 'there' for them. I think everything is in our brain and there is no 'there' somewhere," Maria commented.

"Well what do you mean there is nothing out 'there'?" Innocenti asked.

"What I am saying is that everything is only in our brain and maybe there is no reality out there, like maybe we even have sex in our brain," Maria said.

"Well yes the sensation of having sex is in our brain, but you know something, that 'thing' is a real 'thing' has to go some 'where' in another real 'thing', you know what I mean my sweetheart, right?" Innocenti played.

"Well yeah exactly, that is precisely what I mean. Everything, even those buildings out there, they may not have a reality of their own and they may really exist only in our brain," Maria said thoughtfully.

"Well for example, we know that we live in our house, right here. It has walls and a concrete base. Is this a reality you are denying that exists? The building has a reality of its own outside of our brain. Imagine if we were not around looking at it. Would the building not be there? That is insane to think that the building appears and disappears whether we observe it or not. Imagine if the Moon, this beautiful God-given Moon appearing and disappearing simply because we look at it or not. Furthermore Maria, billions of people may look at it at the same time, so what happens then?" Innocenti asked with care.

"I am saying that we sense everything through our brain and our senses, even when we touch it, like it is just a sensation in our brain. It's the electromagnetic waves that makes us aware of things around us and without the electromagnetic waves absolutely none of our senses would even work and we could not even communicate or know that another world is out there. We would not become aware of our own existence," Maria said with confidence and continued. "You know, in quantum physics, the moment you measure or observe something…you change it, and therefore you never know with 100 percent accuracy the information about that something you tried to measure before measuring or observing it. So once you want to know anything about it you change its characteristics. I am not even sure of the accuracy of measurement because there is no 'exact sciences' but there is a hidden secret about the physical world that we can never ever unravel," Maria explained as her inner thoughts and all she had read spilled out of her.

She knew that Quantum Mechanics applied to the subatomic or atomic level size and not necessarily to the bigger objects, but still wanted to tease Innocenti, and was having fun.

"Innocenti, let's apply that principle to our biology in this constantly changing and evolving body of ours. Let's take the building as an example. By the time we talked about it our own brain had physically changed. Our cells, their chemicals, the whole thing changed therefore you are not even that same person who had decided to go do the touching," Maria said and pressed on. "Let me ask you another question, what if I had the ability to trigger a sensation of the building in your brain and creating a picture of this building in your brain and created the same touch sensation, even if no such building ever existed," "you would see and feel the same touch sensation, would you not?" "would you then still think a building was out there?" Maria asked.

"Well, we are not scientifically that advanced yet to do things like that," Innocenti replied.

"That is true my love, what if a god or another advanced creature is making those sensations in us right now without all the real world being out there?" Maria asked.

"Well in that case we won't give a damn and accept the fact that our sensations are true," Innocenti replied. "Maria, let's just say Hallelujah, this is too complicated for a simple priest called Innocenti, but I think this dumb preacher can corner you," Innocenti told Maria as if he can check mate her.

"Ok go ahead, my love," Maria replied.

"If you say there is no reality anywhere, how about our brain? It has to be 'there' some 'where' occupying a piece of space. The same brain that you have been so proudly talking about its sensation…isn't that a 'reality' that you are saying does not exist?" Innocenti asked.

"Ok, Hallelujah," Maria replied, trying to finish the discussion as she acted like she lost the main argument. But did she?

"Oh Maria, I forgot to tell you that an attorney called me last week and asked me to go see him so and I did. I went to his office and had a lengthy talk," Innocenti told her.

"An attorney? Why and what for?" Maria asked, surprised.

"Well, he told me that we may have some information that will help them with a criminal case, a murder mystery case, actually," Innocenti replied.

"What? a murder case? Strange! Who did you kill my innocent Innocenti?" Maria asked jokingly.

"Don't even talk like that! It makes me more nervous. The attorney told me that this couple who have been in the center of it all really need help. He wants us to go to their house to see how we can help them," Innocenti told her.

"Oh ok, we are always ready to get to meet other good people anyway," Maria replied. "It is always good to bring new people to your church. New people…more donations," Maria included. "Aren't you excited to get to know new people? You seem a bit nervous and uncertain about it."

"Oh no, not at all, but I have never liked talking and dealing with attorneys. He gave me their address, the names, Buzz and Mary Armstrong, and he gave me the day and time to go to their house," Innocenti said.

So Innocenti and his wife go to see Buzz and Mary at their house. Let's do another Quantum Jump and listen in.

The doorbell of the Armstrong's rings…Ding-Dong. Mary opens the door, Buzz is watching and notices two people, a lady and a man at the door, he is shocked when he basically sees himself at the door.

'Oh my god,' Buzz is thinking, 'Who in the world is that? Must be my twin. That is me cut in half.' He goes to the bathroom to brush his hair. Mary is also shocked to see Innocenti as well, but asked them to come in.

"Hello everyone," says Mary as she invites both in. Innocenti and Maria say hello to Mary in return and come in as Mary welcomes them into the house and says, "Come in everyone. Have a seat please.".

"Strange...I see my picture on the mantle. How in the world did you get my picture, Mary? I know some people want to be inviting and nice to their guests and they put the guest's picture somewhere for the guest to feel at home," Innocenti said.

"Oh no Mr. Cristo, that's Buzz my husband, he will come to see you both in a second," Mary said. She steps away from the guests a little and calls, "Hey Buzz, our guests are here. Don't be shy. They are waiting to see you."

Buzz comes to the room and meets his twin brother and Maria, and greets them saying, "hello Mr. Cristo, hello Maria." Buzz is shocked to see Innocenti and the resemblance between them.

"Hi Buzz... and please...there is no Mr. Cristo here. My name is Innocenti. Not that I am that innocent, but nice to have seen you," Innocenti said, trying to lighten the room.

"I am shocked to see myself in you," said Buzz, slowly.

"I am only sort of shocked. I had been told that I probably had a twin brother, but I never tried to find you, and I never thought that I would be finding you this way. This is exciting. I am so happy. Come here Buzz and gimme a long warm hug," Innocenti urged.

They continued after holding to each other, a heartfelt hug.

"No telling, you and I are identical twins, absolutely. I have no doubt. I know I was adopted by my loving parents. The only parents I know," Buzz said.

"So was I, Innocenti said and continued. I was found in a basket flowing down a slow-moving river. That's how I was found by my family who adopted me. The kindest parents one could ask for. They are such a nice God-fearing Italian couple," Innocenti said, being so proud of his parents.

"Is that how you ended up with the name Innocenti?" Buzz asked.

"Yes brother, apparently I looked innocent to them," Innocenti remarked with a small laugh.

"Well, your brother Buzz does not look so innocent to me," Mary said jokingly.

"I am not," Buzz said, "but we know that Mary is innocent, and that is the murder mystery that we need to solve," Buzz said.

"What murder mystery?" Maria asked.

"Well, let's talk about it as we are eating. Mary honey, is the dinner ready?" Buzz asked, as he continued talking to Innocenti and Maria about the case.

"Mary has fixed the best Italian dish for you guys since she kind of guessed that you are Italian and has fixed the most famous Italian dish…'Pasta Alla Carbonara', prepared with ingredients with Pecorino cheese, covered with good hot black pepper," Buzz said.

"Mary, you didn't have to go through the trouble! A simple pizza would have been fine with us," Innocenti said.

"Oh no not at all, no problem," Mary commented as she went to get the food ready and arrange the table.

As Mary was getting the food ready to be served Buzz briefed Innocenti and Maria a bit more about the detail of the case and how Mary was charged and how she is out on bail.

"Oh my goodness. How bizarre and unfortunate," Innocenti commented.

"Well what can I say? Yes, bizarre it is, but we have a good attorney with a great team, and they are working on the case, but we know we have an uphill battle," Buzz said.

"Yes, your attorney called me and talked to me about it a bit," Innocenti said.

The two families went on to have the delicious Italian dish and talked about the case. They became good friends and continued to meet and talk with each other. They got their DNA tested to make sure they were indeed twins, even though they really had no doubt that they were identical twins.

The following week they were having dinner at Buzz's house again and they started talking about how they, Innocenti and Maria, could be of help to his brother Buzz and Mary. Their attorney was also present.

During the meeting, as it is normal when attorneys ask questions, Mr. Dershowitz started asking questions about Innocenti's life, marriage, education and little by little became more aggressive questioning Innocenti's whereabouts on the day of the murder.

"Mr. Cristo we really appreciate the fact that you are willing to work with us and to give us more information. Would you mind telling us where you were on the day the murder happened? I believe it was on April 15, the so-called Tax Day," Abel stated.

"Well, I know I was somewhere on our blue planet Earth…this loving Earth that our father has created. I am sure of that, but why do you ask me that question?" Innocenti said, with curiosity in his voice.

"We are not trying to connect you to this unfortunate murder at all," Dershowitz replied.

"I hope not, I'd be real upset if you even tried," Innocenti interjected. "And I therefore refuse to answer that question," He finished, with a raised voice.

"But honey, we are here to help them. Why would you mind telling them where you were on that day?" Maria asked.

"Well can we meet at your office, Mr. Dershowitz? I really want to help you, but there are things in life that one may not want to share so casually. Especially when it comes to a murder case. I know women usually get so sensitive about legal questions, and as you can see my wife Maria is already stressed out, so let me have my attorney and I meet with you in your office. How about that?" suggested Innocenti.

"But I want to be there," Maria said abruptly and emphatically.

"Honey, that is not a good place for you to be in. You are a very emotional person. I promise to keep you posted with all the details," Innocenti told Maria.

Maria, not knowing what is going on really gets upset. She is wondering why there is a talk about a murder, why there are attorneys involved, and why it is that her own husband is so nervous about all of this. She thinks in their simple life there should not be a place for discussing a murder case, but why is Innocenti evading and not answering some simple questions, she wonders.

"That is not a good start between two brothers," Innocenti told Buzz. "When I saw you, I felt such a deep inner pleasure to have found my twin and *now* this type of questioning by your attorney?" Innocenti commented.

"Well brother, I really don't want you to think that we are trying to connect you in any way to this murder, but we need any help we can get from you," Buzz said.

"Well, then what is this nonsense and this line of questioning about my whereabouts?" Innocenti asked flatly.

Buzz quickly answered, trying to control the heavy emotions. "Let's all calm down. We all know that Mary is charged with a murder and she knows she is innocent, and I believe her...not that we want to say that you brother, may have committed this awful murder, but since my DNA has been found at the murder scene and your blood is almost certainly the same as mine as the DNA test will definitely show, I have no doubt that they will look at you as another suspect. And we want to make sure that you won't be looked at that way…that is all Abel was trying to establish,"

"This is crazy, insane, nonsense," Innocenti said as he stood up madly. Maria, let's go honey. This is bunch of garbage they are telling us! I can't believe they are asking us to answer their crazy questions,"

They left without a family hug. Buzz was saddened to see his brother leaving them like that. Mary is so happy though thinking, 'Is Innocenti the murderer?'

In their car on the way home Innocenti and Maria talked about the case. Maria was a bit puzzled about Innocenti's evasive answers, but she kept quiet as if not talking about it the case would go away. The following day Innocenti, without Maria meets with the attorney, but Buzz was present in the meeting. Innocenti had asked his attorney to go with him.

"Mr. Dershowitz, I brought my attorney with me, Mr. Johnson," Innocenti tells Dershowitz.

"Hello Mr. Johnson, I am Abel Dershowitz," The attorney states.

"Nice to have met you, I am Po Johnson. Call me Po…that is my nick name… not that I am poor but that is what I am called, especially in my professional work and in courts," Po Johnson says.

"What is your real name, if I may ask?" Abel questions.

"That is a long story, and I prefer that we just get on with the case," Po replied, trying to exercise some control and get the upper hand over Dershowitz.

"Ok, everyone knows about the case and we just wanted to have an informal meeting to see how we can help to solve this murder mystery. Alternatively, we can do it in a more formal way, if you prefer of course, and subpoena Mr. Cristo and his wife to come in and be questioned under oath. All we want to prove is that Mrs. Armstrong is innocent of the murder charge," Dershowitz said.

"That is all good and dandy, but not at the expense of my client. Mr. Cristo has told me about your aggressive line of questioning about his whereabouts the day of the murder," Po commented.

"Oh no, not at all, but we don't want to get the DA involved with this, at least not now," Dershowitz said.

"Mr. Cristo, now that you have your attorney with you, let me ask you once again, were you in that city that day…the day of the murder?" Questioned Mr. Dershowitz, calmly.

"I have had a brain operation and my memory fails at times, so I don't re-member the exact date but yes, I was there in that city…I think around that day," Innocenti replied.

"Can I ask you what you were doing there?" Mr. Dershowitz pressed.

Innocenti got a bit nervous being asked that question, but there was no way out and he had to give an answer.

"Would you mind sir, if my client and I leave your office for a few minutes and go to the lobby and talk?" Mr. Johnson asks.

They go to the lobby and talk for a few minutes, in an exceptionally low voice.

"You know Innocenti, I thought that maybe they were recording us. That is why I asked for *us* to leave the room and not Abel. I noticed that you were getting nervous and I thought you wanted to disclose something important that I was not aware of," Po wonders aloud to Innocenti.

"Yes, I was nervous. You know I was there that day, and I met this woman, but I didn't want the attorney to know that," declares Innocenti, in a hushed voice.

"What is going on Innocenti? Maybe we should have talked about the case a little more in detail before we came here. I didn't think that you had any re-mote connection with this murder. What are these new revelations? Not good, not good at all," Po commented out of frustration.

"Well, it is a long story, but briefly, this woman called me and said she wanted to make a confession. She said it was extremely important for me to meet her," Innocenti disclosed to him.

"But why in that city? Why couldn't she come to you?" Po interjected in confusion.

"Well, she said that she could not come to my town, hours away. She told me that she didn't know what to tell her husband. Apparently she wanted to make a confession about an affair and also about a potential twin of mine, so I did not tell my wife about the trip but told her that I had to stay at the church that night…I know…I lied. I should not have," Innocenti finishes, dis-appointed in himself and the position he is in.

"What did the woman tell you?" Po asked.

"She told me that she had a short sexual affair with a person that looked exactly like me and that she imagined that he was my twin…and also that the person was an astronaut," Innocenti said, quietly.

"An astronaut?" Po asked, amazed. "And how did she know how *you* looked like?"

"Apparently she knew me from a few years back attending my church before she moved out of my city," Innocenti answered.

"But why didn't you want your wife to know?" Po questioned.

"Po, you know how *women* are. Had I told her that I needed to go to another city and meet a woman, you know what would have happened, don't you?" Innocenti explains and questions.

Is Innocenti lying? Maybe he had an affair with the lady and is fabricating the story, or maybe he is the killer of Anna and the rest of his story is just a smoke screen. Po and Innocenti go back to the room and tell the story to Abel after having asked Buzz to leave the room. They did not want to get Buzz all upset disclosing his alleged affair. Buzz was upset when he was asked to leave the room, thinking, 'what a mess, what is going on here?'

They all go through some more questions and answers. Some involved Mary and some, Innocenti.

After the meeting ends, Po and Innocenti meet separately. Dershowitz tells Buzz and asks for his consent for him to call the DA office and disclose the new findings and to give the DA contact information for Innocenti and Maria. Abel also very briefly tells Buzz about the affair allegation and Buzz categorically denies it.

Now let's Quantum Jump to the DA office, where they are meeting with the case prosecutor and some attorneys.

"We have some fresh clues about our mystery case," the DA starts. "This man, Innocenti Cristo, is apparently the identical twin of Buzz Armstrong. After all his wife may not be the main suspect, or not a suspect at all. Innocenti Cristo is apparently Buzz's identical twin and we need to get his blood sample and do our own DNA test and not just rely on the looks of the two. We have to make sure the DNA exactly matches the blood found at the murder scene. We can't lose this case or make an ass out of ourselves. The whole world is watching us. We have fresh blood to test," The DA finishes.

"But where did the skin tissue come from?" The assistant DA asked.

"We don't know, and I don't believe there is any collusion between Innocenti and Mary, even though they were both in that city on the day of the murder," The DA replied.

So, the prosecutors and attorneys do all the prep work and call Innocenti to come in for an interview. It will be an exciting meeting, for the DA of course, but it will be a complete disaster for Innocenti. The DA and his attorneys meet with Innocenti and is attorney.

"We are so happy to see you, Mr. Cristo and Mr. Johnson. We're so glad that you have come forward with some new information to help us solve this extremely unique murder case that has puzzled us all," Said the DA.

"We are also very happy to be here and hopefully we can shed some lights on the case," Innocenti replied.

"We know that you are the priest of a local Church, a man of God, and we appreciate all the good work you have done for the community. Everyone in town talks good of you, but as you know we have a murder case and your brother's attorney has provided us with some additional information. That's why we have asked you to come in and we thank you so much," The DA said and continued. "It is our procedure, and I am sure your attorney knows this and may have already told you that we have to read you a Miranda warning," The DA said.

Innocenti got a bit puzzled and nervous. Po tells Innocenti to remain quiet and let them read the Miranda warning.

After the Miranda warning is read and some basic questions asked, Po suggests that he needs more time to get prepared for this case and they asked the DA to let them go without answering more question and to set up another meeting. They all agreed and the following day, Innocenti meets Po in his office.

"Innocenti, as your attorney I absolutely need to know everything about this case and your potential involvement with it and you have to be very honest with me and tell me the whole story about your life, your relationship with your wife, and about this woman who made the confession. I know this lady will be causing a nightmare for you. I can see it coming. For example, when you went to that city did you go to the park where the woman was murdered," Po asked.

"Yes," Innocenti replied, sheepishly.

"Why, damn it?! Why in that park? Your DNA has been found at the murder scene and there is you in that park. This is not good news. We cannot claim that it was your brother's blood since he was orbiting the Earth that day," Po commented.

"Yes, but I am telling you the truth and I have nothing to hide, for God's sake. I am not a killer! I am a kind person," Innocenti says, trying to reassure Po.

"Do you have any contact information about the woman who had an affair with Buzz? We may need to talk to her before anyone else does. Not that we want to coach her," Po added carefully.

"Well, I know I have her telephone number in my cell phone, and actually it was so easy I remember it," Said Innocenti as he began jotting down the number on a note pad.

"How did you meet her in the park?" Po asked.

"To be honest with you, I forgot to take my cell phone with me. I mistakenly left it in my church, but I remembered her phone number so when I got there I went to a local supermarket and used their phone and called her so I would be able to meet her," Innocenti explained.

"Oh goodness, now the DA thinks that you had intentionally left your phone not to be tracked. You did it this way, they think, so that if your whereabouts were tracked, supposedly you were in your own town and not in the city where the murder happened. To crown it all, you left it at the church so that your wife would not answer any calls, especially from that woman," Po said as he sounded more concerned.

"Oh no, I assure you that this was not the case. I never have and never will cheat on my wife," Innocenti said seriously.

"I know that you're telling me the truth, but they don't know that. They are after a murderer…a nasty killer…and any clue they can find they will follow. Unfortunately, many of the clues are pointing to you and in their mind you *are* that nasty killer," Po said trying to encourage him to be truthful. "Did you get any gas on the way? Can they see you in any video in any gas station?" Po asked.

"Oh no, as a matter of fact I got gas here in town before I went. I have a gas guzzler. I even got an extra gallon of gas in a container. I kept it in the trunk of my car when I went there," Innocenti explained, trying to disclose the truth to his attorney.

"Don't tell me that. One bad news after another. I can't believe what I am hearing, but they can probably track your whereabouts from your car's GPS anyway, even if they don't see you in any video pumping gas on the way," Po said.

Innocenti looked hopeful and explained some more details saying, "Well no, the good news is that my car tracking was not…,"

"Did you disengage it?...Did you mess with it?" Po abruptly asked before Innocenti could finish his sentence.

"Oh no, it has not been working for some time," Innocenti replied.

"I think we are in deep trouble, Innocenti, and the skin is our only hope. You haven't had any injury lately, have you?" Po asks with concern.

"What trouble? I don't understand your concern Po. why am I or should I be in trouble?" Innocenti presses.

"I think you will be charged with the murder," Po explains carefully. "This is the way the prosecutors push people to provide additional information and get conviction. They charge them first. And based on what I know so far, the skin tissue is your brother's skin. I hope you have not had any injury in the past month or so and especially on that date. The only credible defense we have is that Buzz's skin was in there, and because of your brother's cut, it will be against Mary and not you," Po added, with a bit of confidence. "I will give them hell if they charge you. They have to go through my tough stand,"

"Po, I don't want to disappoint you but now that you asked I have to be honest with you. I did cut my hand that same day, and in that park. The lady was so nice, she had brought a couple of apples and started peeling them. She turned to give me a couple of cut apples as we were sitting on a bench and accidentally hit me with the knife...and a part of my finger was cut off. She had an old Swiss Army knife, so it was not a huge deep cut and no stitches were needed, but some skin came off. The knife fell on the ground and I picked it up and gave it to her. She said she was a nurse and she quickly cleaned the blood and the skin from my hand. She was going to dispose of them 'properly' she said. She was a very caring person...I could feel that," Innocenti explained.

Po couldn't believe what he was hearing, and his thoughts began to take over. "Oh my God, one evidence after another is showing up. God help us. With my long standing as a good attorney and my perfect winning statistics I don't even know if I should try this case. Maybe I should drop it and carry on with my life. Should I worry about my reputation?" Po thought that there is no way they could win this case.

Po tried to push his thoughts away and continued discussing what their defense strategy should be, again asking Innocenti if he really was 100% innocent. Po told him the odds were staggered against him, but that Innocenti not to be concerned or sympathetic towards Mary, and that his only concern should be about himself.

Now let's Quantum Jump to Buzz's house and see what is going on with them.

Buzz, Mary, and Abel Dershowitz held several strategy meetings discussing the detail and how they will go about proving Mary's innocence. With the story about Innocenti's involvement they have new hopes, but Buzz's feeling is bittersweet, with his wife on one side and Innocenti on the other.

"Mary let me ask you a few questions," Abel started. "Tell me, when Buzz cut his hand how did you clean it and how did you dispose of the skin tissue and blood? Did you put the skin tissue in the garbage can, the garbage disposal or where?" he asked.

"Well, I put them both in a Ziplock bag and in our garbage can. Any problem with that?" Mary asked.

Abel tried not to look concerned and replied, "It all depends, who collects your garbage, is it the city or a private company?"

"It's a private company," Mary replied.

"Have you guys ever had any conflicts with the garbage collector or the driver?" Abel pressed.

"Yes, as a matter of fact, they missed taking our garbage twice in a row. The third time Buzz went to the curbside and was waiting for them. They argued about it and the driver got physically involved with Buzz. The two of them, the driver and the garbage guy, struggled for a few minutes. But my husband being much stronger, they backed off. They were so mad and as they were leaving they started yelling at Buzz telling him that they will get even with him," Mary said dramatically.

"That is extremely important, and it could have a big impact on our case," Abel said with a pause. "However, we don't want to bring another person in as a suspect and then mess anything up since our allegation should be credible," Abel commented.

"I could have put them both down in a second," Buzz said proudly. "But I don't think the garbage man would go through our garbage to find things like that though, do you?"

"Oh yes, they do that all the time," exclaimed Abel. "Not necessarily the garbage collectors, but regular people go through the trash of others to collect financial and personal information and if your garbage man has seen blood and skin that is all he needed to frame you," Abel finished, so confidently.

"For goodness sake, I can't believe the garbage guys would be so mean," Buzz retorted.

"Did you report the struggle to the police?" Abel asked Buzz.

"Oh no, it was not a real fight and just a little struggle. As I said, I could have put them down easily but because of my job I gave it a very low effort. Otherwise it would have been on the news…an astronaut assaulting a little garbage man, can you imagine? The news anchors would have loved to make some money out of it, I bet. But you know what?" Asked Buzz, with a questioned look on his face. "I think we were the last house in our big subdivision, so possibly there would not have been any additional garbage that went over ours. So it would have been extremely easy to go through and mess with ours," Buzz told Abel.

"Well, we need to tell this to the district attorney since it is a very significant finding for them to chew on. They will have to be followed and checked out," Dershowitz stated.

"Abel, is this going to get my charges reversed?" Mary asked, with some new hope.

"No, not so quickly," Abel replied. "We have a long way to go for that. Let's get the DA to do another DNA test of the skin and see if they can determine if it matches your brother's, and also what part of the body it came from. Is it from the hand, the arm, or even the skull? They can do that by looking at the stem cells. Of course, if any stem cell was included in the skin they are holding on to. I'll make that request,"

"So, you think the garbage man can become a suspect?" Buzz asked.

"Yes, that is exactly where I am going with this. We have to find out if by any chance they have been in that city on that day," Abel replied.

Mary feels some relief realizing that the DA may look at the garbage collectors. She talks to Dershowitz again and answers some other questions.

Abel goes to the DA and explains the situation one more time. He talks about the fact that a garbage collector could have had access to Buzz's skin and blood. This combined with the physical entanglement with Buzz and the threat made by the garbage collector threatening to get even are all clues to be followed up by the DA office. The DA asked the attorney how the garbage collector would know that this was Buzz's blood anyway. Abel told him that the blood was from this house and the garbage man didn't care if it was his or his wife's, presuming he just wanted revenge.

Abel had previously asked the DA office to have the skin tested and see if the skin were that of a hand or somewhere else in the body, as he thought that would also be significant.

Abel had told the DA that Mary went to that city but did not disclose it in an effort not to embarrass Buzz. Apparently, the lady whom Mary met in that town wanted to confide an affair with Buzz. She wanted to personally tell this to Mary, to apologize and ask for forgiveness. She told Mary that she was devastated, and that it was a one-night stand and assured her the affair ended quickly. This "allegedly" happened when Buzz had gone to that city and met her at a bar late at night.

She apparently knew Buzz because she had followed the news on space missions. She had also known Innocenti as a church leader and thought they were twins but did not know that the two brothers did not know about each other and were not aware of them being twins. So, when Innocenti met with her she told Innocenti about his potential brother Buzz, the astronaut. That is why when Innocenti met Buzz for the first time Buzz was so shocked, but Innocenti was not.

For you and me to find out who Anna's killer is, should we not ask ourselves as to why Buzz got a call from Chima's President when Mary was charged? Why should Chima's President be so concerned?.

Well the result of the skin test came, even though the skin had come off the hand it had traces of new growth and some nucleotides were different than those of Buzz's DNA. The lab and the DNA expert working with the DA office had reported that finding. The blood DNA had all traces of hereditary signature and matched with that of Buzz, just with the difference in the sequence of nucleotides in the DNA, which could have been the result of mutations, the effect of chemical molecules in the body, exposure to the Sun, or perhaps other reasons. The mitochondrial DNA that had come from their mother also matched.

"I will bring all sorts of DNA experts and will give the prosecutor hell. We will get you off the hook Mary," Abel said, having new ammunition to work with.

With all these new findings Dershowitz asks the DA office to again compare the skin and blood DNA with those of Innocenti. They did that and the result came in and matched with the blood of Innocenti much more than with the blood of Buzz. The DA calls Dershowitz and informs him of the result. The prosecutor had also talked to the woman who had an affair with Buzz and the detail of her meeting with Mary. The lady told the DA that her meeting with Mary was all about confessing to her the facts of her affair with Buzz. After the DA office talks to the woman he clears Mary's name and informs them right away.

"Buzz, come here honey! The DA office just called! I knew it, I knew it and I knew it! They have cleared my name! This is absolutely the best news ever! Let's celebrate tonight with Champagne!" Mary exclaimed to Buzz with the biggest smile on her face.

She screamed with joy and really cherished the news. She acted like she was a victim, but was she? Has the DA been fooled? And we ask again why did the President of Chima call Buzz? Another mystery added to our murder mystery, and we should think about that.

Nonetheless, Mary and Buzz celebrated that night. It was a cheerful and happy night, yet now Buzz was a bit concerned about his twin brother, Innocenti. Mary and Buzz received a congratulatory call from their attorney Dershowitz.

The DA calls Innocenti and his attorney and ask him some questions about his whereabouts and learn much more about Innocenti's involvement. They are extremely happy, as they think Innocenti is their man. Two hours of questioning helped the DA, and many questions and answers helped them to form their opinion.

Now the DA's focus and attention go on Innocenti. They have the skin and blood found at the murder scene matching with Innocenti's in their DNA blood database. He had gone to the city that same day where the murder happened as per his own confession, and as a matter of fact he was in the same remote park where the murder took place. He had left his phone not to be tracked and he had his car GPS possibly tampered with. He had bought gas in his hometown so that he would not have to get gas on the way. He even had bought extra gas just in case he runs out of gas on his way home. He had this well planned, and quite delicately and carefully executed. He was a smart planner, a premeditated killer. He is their man...a murderer...as per the DA office, of course.

But since we don't have a confession, we don't know who the real killer is, do we? We can only guess. Our guess may also be indicating that Innocenti is the killer. But with good attorneys and experts can the DA bring a final conviction?

The DA told his assistants "we got him" and that they had their crime solved and had their man. They quickly take the case to a Grand Jury and get them to agree to charge Innocenti. That was an easy task with the evidence building up against him. He had become their fall man, a priest murderer in their files.

They call him and give him the shocking news and ask him to turn himself in. He is devastated. He tells Maria and then calls his parents to tell them the story as well. They are mentally destroyed when they hear the news. He asks the DA's office to call his attorney to tell him exactly why he was being charged. The DA calls Po and explains why Innocenti should turn himself in. Po, not being surprised, calls Innocenti and tells him to follow the DA's instruction. He promises to put up a good fight.

Maria is crying as Innocenti screams, "Why, why Me?"

Maria tries to calm him down and declares, "My love, we all know you are innocent, and your God knows that. We have one of the top attorneys in the country and he has a strong team working on your case. I have no doubt that no jury will convict you," Maria said and continued. "You are so well known to be the kindest man in town. You have done so much charitable works here and you'll have thousands of people sign affidavits supporting you. They will come to the court and be your character witness,"

Innocenti looks defeated but tries to press on in answering. "I know that honey, but for the DA that does not amount to a hill of beans. In their mind I am a liar, a killer, and a cheater to start with and I have to prove my innocence. And if I don't I'll be tortured, bankrupted and at the end my head will be gone. That is exactly what they did to my Jesus and what did my innocent Jesus do to be killed so savagely?"

Suddenly the phone rings and Maria answers it quickly. It is her father-in-law.

"Hi sweetie, this is John...how are you? I have some good news, I hope. You may have already seen the news on TV. The DA office mistakenly leaked the news that they had found the murder weapon, a knife, a Swiss Army knife, they said so far they have seen just a trace of blood on it and are examining the fingerprint, they are still doing further checks. It is strange, but there is some trace of sugar on the knife as well they say. I am sure this will give my innocent son some relief. Please let him know, okay? And I don't need to tell you this, but we will do our best to pay for the attorney fees, even if we have to sell our house. Not much equity in it, but what the heck… this is about Innocenti. We love you all. Give Innocenti a big hug for us," John tells Maria.

"Oh great. Yes, that's good news John. Let me rush and tell him that," Maria replied.

"Honey, it was your dad on the phone with some good news for us," Maria says, rushing back into the room.

"Oh? What good news?" He asked.

"They have found the murder weapon, they think…a knife…trace of blood on it. Apparently they had this, but the news was somehow leaked to the media by mistake. Anyway, they are checking or confirming the fingerprint, Apparently a Swiss Army knife," Maria finishes, out of breath.

"Oh my God, I really don't want to talk about that… not right now," Innocenti says, still obviously defeated and feeling bad for himself.

Why did the words "Swiss Army knife" make him so nervous? He knows what that means: Bad, bad news, again and again.

A few weeks passed for the paperwork to find its slow move through the justice system and Innocenti to be tried.

The DA having charged Innocenti, freed on bail for now, goes for the kill. They go in with the highest penalty. First Degree Murder…premeditated, and therefore they ask for the death penalty by lethal injection. Innocenti is in deep, deep you know what!

The news of his charge and potential conviction devastated the church. The church leaders discuss it with their members, they hold many prayer meetings for Innocenti. The membership drops way down. Because of the loan the church had obtained to expand their building they had no choice but to file for bankruptcy protection.

During the trial there were ups and downs for Innocenti and with all the good attorneys that he had the Jury convicts him of first-degree murder and the presiding Judge imposes the sentence, capital punishment, death by injection under the State code.

Po filed an appeal and persuaded the court that Innocenti was no danger to the society and there was no flight risk. Many of the Church members call the Judge and become his character witnesses. The court ordered Innocenti to wear an electronic tracking device and not to be allowed to travel outside of the city. They also took away his passport as a precondition.

While his case is on appeal Po Johnson and his team of attorneys meet many times and discuss the case and they even ask for Dershowitz to assist them. Due to conflict of interest he refers his brother, a high-class sharp attorney, to help Po Johnson. The brother, Dwight Dershowitz agrees to take the case provided he will be in charge and to take the lead. It is now them versus the whole power of the State and the United States government bearing down on their case. You can imagine with all these attorney bills; this family is going into debt.

Po and Dwight Dershowitz ask Innocenti to do some fundraising for his defense team. He tries and although he does his best, not much money comes in. He goes for an internet fundraiser, but even that was not successful and attorney bills are piling up on him.

"Honey what are we going to do? I swear on my beloved Jesus, that I am innocent...it is just that I cannot prove it. How are we going to pay for all these attorney bills? I'd rather die than pile up so much unpaid bills on you. I don't want to sell our house and wonder where are you going to live when I am gone?" Innocenti says, broken down.

"Oh, honey you aren't going anywhere, but let's ask our best friend, Ben to help. He has a trademark on his name of 'BCASSO© as if he can paint like Pablo Picasso, but he has been very successful, his paintings are going for millions of dollars. Do you think he will help?" Maria asked.

"Well, I know he has a kind heart and we can try. Do you think he will help though? That is a lot of money. Seven hundred thousand dollars, so far," Innocenti said.

"Worth trying," Mary replied.

So Innocenti calls Ben and asks him to come over. He does, right away.

"Hi Ben, my God I have not seen you for a while," Innocenti said.

"I know, how in the world have you been? I have heard the news and I was about to call you and see if I could help," Ben said.

"Well, that is one of the reasons we asked you to come over," Innocenti admitted quickly. "I need some money to defend myself. Do you think you can give us a loan of some 700,000 dollars? Just a loan, Ben…and I promise to pay you back. You know, these attorneys are charging me over 600 dollars an hour. Ridiculous! And believe me, Ben…I have thought about killing myself a few times. We can sell our house and my parents are selling theirs but that will not help much to pay the debt off,"

"Oh my god, Innocenti…you realize that you are asking for 700,000 dollars from me, right?" Ben asked.

"Yes, and I am ashamed of myself asking for that. Believe me I will pay you back. I am innocent. I know that my church people will come to my help," Innocenti says, with all the remaining hope he can muster.

"Well, let me tell you something. 700,000 dollars is a lot of money, you know that don't you?" Ben asked.

"We do my friend, we do," Innocenti and Mary confirmed.

"Well, my friendship with you and Maria goes back for many years. So not only will I give you that amount, but I will put in your account another 1 million dollars. That's what friends are for isn't it? I have been a successful oil paint artist and my paintings are going for millions of dollars, so no problem my friend. I spend an hour doing a crazy style painting and some insane people pay a million dollars for it. They think after I am dead that they can sell those for billions, so not a big deal. Come here Innocenti just gimme a hug my friend," Says Ben, nodding to his friend.

After Innocenti and Maria thanked Ben they further discussed the case and how they will appeal it. Some three months passed.

Let's do another Quantum Jump and go to the office of the director of FBI. The office of FBI Director, Jack C. Nikola opens and this Chinese looking man has been brought in with some fresh information to inform the FBI on a potential disaster brewing up. After he introduced himself, he asked for anonymity and was given the designation "TC". He had just come to the United States and at the airport had applied for political asylum, telling the U.S. government that he had some information about a potential disaster and the killing of Anna Rodriguez.

"We really appreciate your concern and willingness to share with us and providing us with some information Mr. TC. We don't want to start asking you questions and prefer that you give us what you will voluntarily," Jack Ni-kola said.

"I just had to do this Mr. Nikola, it concerns me so much and I was left with no other choice and doing this goes against my own national principles. I am Chimese and going against my own country is not something that I ever, ever wanted to do, but I am a person who believes in God so killing and tor-turing people, or potentially killing millions of people is not a Godly thing to me so that is why I am here sir. I did apply for political asylum and I hope my government does not find out about it. If they do I will be killed by my own government," TC explained carefully and continued.

"The communist country of Chima wants to rule the world. They have fig-ured out how to accomplish that, they think. They have been planning for this for a very long time. They have to end the U.S. first and most probably the Western countries in Europe, Canada, India, Japan and Australia. Providing food for 1.3 billion Chinese people and growing is their main concern. They know that nu-clear war is expensive, and it causes mutual destruction, so what is the easiest, least expensive plan? It will be biological and going after the economy of the western countries. They are sure that during that process even drowning a navy ship in the South Chima Sea won't trigger a major war. They are willing to take that risk,"

"Being in high positions within the Chimese government I know a lot, but I also have a few close agents who will come to the United States soon and will apply for political asylum. We will need their information on a regular basis, and we want their constant updates. Let me be in touch with them through my sources and I will feed you any information I will receive," TC said with seriousness.

"I will go back and forth to Chima to make everything appear normal and because they already have so many installed agents here I have to be careful, tracking people is their expertise. They call me every other hour or on a sur-prise basis and I have to answer my phone...otherwise they will suspect some-thing is out of ordinary. I had to leave my phone next door in a hotel so I can come in and out of here very quickly," TC finished.

Without being specific, TC very vaguely talked about some vaccine pro-duction and repositioning of some satellites by Chima claiming that he cannot disclose and be more specific at this time. After some additional data that TC provided, they had concluded their meeting.

The FBI is incredibly happy for his cooperation but also worried about the information TC gave. They start following him constantly. As it is a norm, the FBI start a FISA court process to be able to listen to his conversation. However, they are not sure that TC is being truthful, especially since he will go back and forth to Chima, his home country. They don't want to disclose any information to TC but just to receive information. Now this is another indication about satellites being repositioned and now talking about a bio attack. Is a bio attack really in the works?

Because the information was about a bio attack and satellites being repositioned the military heads assembled a task force of 200 military and communications experts including the heads of CDC and the Space Force. They assembled a huge monitoring room with the latest live real time data available to them. The President will be briefed on a daily or hourly basis.

Let's Quantum Jump again and listen in as TC meets with the FBI director. He is of course being recorded and he knows that. Is he truthful or is this a trick played by Chima with misinformation? Misinformation causes loss of resources and misdirects the attention of government agencies. We have seen that many times over. It is sickening, but true.

"Mr. Nikola I have to give you two pieces of information and cannot go any further. I have in my possession a video of the killing of Anna Rodriguez, but unfortunately the video is in my office in Chima. I can also tell you that 500 satellites, 60 of which are communication satellites, have been repositioned in the past 3 days. Without being more specific, let me just tell you not to forget a code. It is number 10. I repeat…number 10. Very quickly…another piece of information is code DV. The danger is not imminent but will be coming soon," TC declared as he rushed back to his hotel. He again emphasized, for the second time, that viruses actually *do* discriminate.

The task force starts analyzing the new information and gathering more satellite data and on a vaccination. The United States, with so many satellites and capabilities of its own Space Force is now on notice. They quickly start analyzing the available data on Chimese high Earth Orbit, medium Earth Orbit, and low Earth Orbit satellites. Just like when you are in a sports arena, the higher you are sitting, the more you see of the arena. Do we know which country has the highest orbit satellite going around the Earth? Of course, and there lies the danger. But then the higher the orbit, the longer the length of time in communication ability…unless the speed of communication is different and much higher.

The US military puts all their nuclear-powered submarines on highest alert without disclosing it to the public. The U.S. government does not want the public to panic. Not yet. And what did TC mean by number or code 10?

We do know that the satellite's view of the Earth depends on the satellite's height, eccentricity, and inclination, which is the angle between the plane of the orbit and the equator and those can determine the path of the satellites. Eccentricity refers to the orbital shape of the satellite.

Now let us go back to our own exciting story.

Innocenti, Maria, and his parents decided to discuss the detail of the case together. They all go to a Mexican restaurant in Maria's big SUV and talk about the case. On the way back home two police cars stop them, six policemen come out and show their badges and surround them and ask them to go to another SUV. They realize this is not an ordinary arrest and they resist, but they are overcome by six strong policemen and are put in the other SUV.

They ask the scary looking policemen what is going on and they receive nothing but absolute silence. The policemen easily take off Innocenti's ankle bracelet. All their cell phones and the tracking device were handed over to another car's driver who took off quickly. They have been kidnapped and are all taken to a remote location, put in chains, and left in a locked dark room.

Now let's Quantum Jump and hear what is going on with the parents of Anna Rodriguez, who are meeting with a few of their friends and talking about Innocenti. He talks with a heavy broken Spanish accent. But wait…before we do that let's quickly see and hear the latest from TC reporting to the FBI office again.

TC tells the FBI office that Chima has had an evil goal brewing, but after so much theft of technological secrets from the West and U.S. companies they still desperately needed some genetic sequencing specific to some viruses. Somehow, they are still trying to use their agents to steal genetic engineering technology from the west. If they must use threat or buy through bribes, their intention is to do that.

He also talks about a person in an extremely high position in Chima who is like the Gorbachev of the old Soviet Union. This person is sick and tired of the constant violation of human rights in Chima and the unethical theft of intellectual properties from U.S. companies. He thinks this is not the true character of kind Chimese people and he told the FBI that theft is the main strategy of Chima's Communist Party. He leaves some evidence supporting these accusations, including some videos and internal documents, and then TC quickly goes back to his hotel.

So now the FBI not only is getting corroborating information from their own sources through other CIA agents, but now Chinese informers are confirming the same information. Is any kind of danger around the corner?

Let's go back to Anna's father talking to his supporters.

"You know the justice system in this country sickens me. It takes forever to convict someone and bring him to justice. We know that his attorney has appealed his case for the murder of our daughter, but we have him now. He is the killer of my dear Anna and if we let them try to convict him in their court it means years of waiting. Don't they say justice delayed is justice denied? We know what to do with him," Anna's father said, tears coming down his cheeks.

"We want to be fair and we will put him through our real court, just as they do it in their crazy court system, but we do it fast," Anna's mother said.

Their "fair" court system consists of a panel of one Judge, who is Anna's father; one prosecutor who is Anna's uncle, and one Juror, who is Anna's mother. They will give him a so called 'fair' trial by giving him an attorney who is Anna's angry brother. The father says that they have asked the brother not to be angry and give Innocenti a good defense.

The DA hears the news of the kidnapping and friends and the family are devastated. First, they think that Innocenti had escaped but then after reviewing some videos they realized that he and his family were kidnapped. They start looking for them.

Now let's Quantum Jump to their sham court. Anna's father introduces himself and his family to Innocenti.

"Mister Innocenti, my name is José Rodriguez. I am Anna's father and we have brought you here. There are the three of us, me as the Judge, a prosecutor and an honest Juror and of course your wife and parents. This is an extremely fair court…the three of us versus the four of you. We did not want to overwhelm your side with more of our supporters. Thousands of them wanted to come and kill you. We are very fair, you know. We want you to defend yourself. Our agents have learned about your case and we know that your blood and skin have been found at the murder scene of our beloved daughter. She was ruthlessly killed by you. No other person's blood and skin have been found at the murder scene. You killed our daughter and we think you are guilty of this murder. But please present your defense," says Mr. Rodriguez.

"I will let my attorney present my defense first, as I am not familiar with your court system," Innocenti said and stood forward.

As soon as the "defense" attorney started presenting the defense he got emotional and started crying and very quickly…not walked, but ran out of the court room. So now Innocenti must defend himself.

"I don't know what to tell you. They say that the blood is mine, but I don't know who planted it at the murder scene. I went to that city to receive a confession from a lady about a sex affair. I did not kill your daughter. I don't have any other defense. If you believe in justice, then listen to your God and do as you see fit," Innocenti told them and sat down on an unsteady squeaky chair.

"Well your first argument is rejected… the blood is yours. We think you had gone there to have sex with that lady and now you do not want to confess it in front of your wife. Therefore that second defense is also rejected. We think you are giving us a bunch of nonsense and we are one hundred percent sure that you are the killer. Do you have any other defense sir," Innocenti was asked by Mr. Rodriguez, who was shaking in anger.

"I know you want to kill me, and I do not have any other defense, so go ahead with your process, and if killing me will satisfy your anger then there is nothing I can do," Innocenti replied. Maria and the parents scream with objections and outrage, but they are taken out of the room, still in chains.

So Innocenti gets "convicted." They had created the same death chamber exactly the way it is in the United States by the relevant State Department of Corrections. They want to show and pretend how fair they are. The moment comes, everyone in the family is in tears, but they are shackled and have been seated behind glass windows to watch him die, against their own will. So much for Freewill!

Maria is concentrating on her beloved husband's innocence, watching him walking toward the death chamber. Let's go to the glass walled room that Maria and Innocenti's parents are and listen to their outrage and prayers.

"God, help us! I don't want him to die…he is your man. I know he is an innocent man…please show your power. I know there is a killer on the loose somewhere and my innocent husband is being killed," Maria calls loudly on her God to help and her parent begin praying aloud, too.

"God, you know how simple of a life we have had. We now wished that we had not found and adopted Innocenti, our innocent boy. He loves you, and now you are putting him through this, why?" Begs Innocenti's mother, Kristina.

"Take me instead of my boy," Cries Innocenti's father, John.

It is time for me, the writer, and you, the feeler, to Quantum Jump to the utmost inner mind of Innocenti and hear what he is telling himself as he is walking toward the death chamber. Maybe he has fooled us, and he is the killer and he is finally admitting to his God, so he won't be lying to himself in his last moments. Will he ask for mercy? Will he repent for any killing or any sin he has committed? Is this kind of quick justice better than a much longer one? You and I don't think so but when a person's son or daughter is killed it causes so much anger and outrage in the close family. Reasoning vacates any chamber of justice. Isn't this happening in wars when innocent people get killed, thousands at a time…even millions? Where is justice for them? Is this a just world? Is this God's creation?

You and I are now in Innocenti's brain going around and delving into his innermost neuronal networks in different lobes of his brain as he is talking to himself. It is a pure self-conversation, nothing but the truth, 100 billion neurons talking to each other as his brain is active and heating up. Trillions and trillions of proteins in his brain are synching together, neurotransmitters of different kinds are passing through the synapses causing anger and other emotions. Some neurotransmitters are absorbed, some are not and instead they are taken up again.

Let's listen into his self-talk.

"God this is incomprehensible. I wonder, God, what you would do if you were me…innocent, but charged with murder? You and only you know that I am innocent. I don't mind coming to you but please take care of my love, Maria, and my parents. You brought me to this world of yours, gave me a chance to live a good life, and I did. I committed no sins…the sins that *you* had created God. In spite of all the motivations to do bad, I stayed faithful to you. I was a good man, a good husband, a good son to my parents. You gave me a canvas called life. You gave me a brush, colorful thoughts and steady hands. I used them with no wrong. I tried to make each corner of my life's canvas your masterpiece. I watched all my strokes and your every sunrise brought a promise to my life and your every sunset gave me hope for a better tomorrow.

Is there a tomorrow for me to meet you? I have no doubt. I love you God. I love you Jesus. Let them put your chemical in me, yes, the chemicals that *you* have created, I am ready…let me caress you when I see you, but please rush it. Take me as an innocent man…don't wait another second as I may do wrong. I may commit a wrongful thought and become a sinner. I am clean and ready to come to you. Take me to your lap my God…take me now…now," Innocenti prays as he is walking toward the sham court's death chamber.

His sense of dread increases as he is taking each step, and with each step his worried look turns into a happy smile. He has given up. He looks at Maria and his parents through the glass window and sends them a kiss. Innocenti arrives and the curtains now close. There is no one in the room but Anna's parents and revenge is the only thing in their mind.

"Do you have any final wishes?" Ana's father asks Innocenti.

Innocenti responds in peace. "No, not to you, and not even to my God. I have already talked to him. He brought me to this world innocent and is taking me back innocent," He continues with his remarks saying, "God's nature does not make you wonder just sometimes. It makes you wonder always, even upon death. Dying is as magnificent as being born. Send me to my God, send me now. Just know that I did not kill your daughter. Go find the real killer after I am gone," Innocenti makes these last remarks before he is killed.

Innocenti lies on the bed to receive the lethal injection, absolute silence is in every inch of the building, except behind the glass door where Maria and Innocenti's parents are. The clock is ticking. Every second that passes, Innocenti is closer to death.

Before they kill this "innocent" man, you and I can Quantum Jump and appear in Innocenti's brain again but this time we want to look around for ourselves…not to find out about his self-talk…but look into his physical brain…to see if we find anything unusual. After all he has had a brain surgery in the past. We can go around his neuronal network…in different lobes of his brain. Let's take our last opportunity before he is put to death. We saw…we heard…we felt his innocence as he was talking to himself. Nobody was there for him to lie to. You and I move around his brain. They do a brain biopsy after a person is dead…but you and I can do the "biopsy" as he is alive. Ionic pulses all over his brain…billions of neurons working and talking to one another…they use their own chemical language that we don't understand. Each individual neuron is alive...yet we think we are conscious because of their wholesomeness. Information is being coded, decoded and coordinated. How is this man's consciousness at work...we wonder...his brain is the reflection of the world. It sees the world...it feels the world...it understands the world even though it is bunch of chemicals and cells stuck together in the tiniest of space. The world is in his brain. We see some unusual long axons much larger than normal...but why this long we ask. Time is running out, so let us go back and see what is happening to him. But wait...for goodness sake we see a tiny orange color metal device implanted in his brain...so unusual. We remind ourselves...why did the President of Chima call Buzz? We ask ourselves, why was this device put in his brain? Was he being constantly controlled and forced to kill?

The clock is ticking. We wished we could go to Anna's father's brain and persuade him we have seen an unusual metal device in Innocenti's brain. Maybe he did not have or exercise any Freewill of his own even if he did kill Anna. But why would this angry man listen to us? He may think we are crazy, and no evidence will satisfy this man's outrage. All he wants is to kill this Murderer. His daughter will be happy, he thinks.

The moment of his finality has arrived. The chemical tube is connected to his vein...the dead girl's father is about to push the button to release the chemical to go into Innocenti's body. He tells Innocenti that he has ten more seconds in this world.

Innocenti hears the push of the button, he knows that in ten seconds he will meet Anna and his biological parents, if they have died. Will he see his God? He is counting the seconds...

10...

9...

8...

7...

6...

5...

4...

3...

2...

1...

The first drop of the chemical drops and goes to his vein. Another drop goes in. Innocenti will die soon.

The sound of an explosion shakes the building.

"Everyone's hands up, get on the floor!" A shout echoes as twenty SWAT team police members holding machine guns overwhelm the building. The father is thrown on the floor and quickly put in hand cuffs. Innocenti's hand is unhooked from the tube. The building is surrounded by 200 SWAT team members securing the area.

Every one of the gang members are arrested. The police realized that Innocenti could die at any second, so they transport him by helicopter to the closest hospital. The doctors reverse the effect of the chemical with another drug and he survives. His parents are happy and so are Maria and Innocenti. How about Anna's parents? Happy? Heck no, they are outraged! They had lost their daughter and now this?!

Innocenti, Maria, Kristina and John thank the police, but now when will the real trial start? How much are Innocenti and his family supposed to suffer for a murder we are not sure he committed. But let's not forget any Chima connection.

Before we continue with the life of Innocenti and his trial let's quickly go to the office of Mr. Nikola as he meets again with our newly found "friend," TC. Who knows…Could he be a part of the enemy's misinformation structure? Will we eventually find out?

"I only have a minute or two! I have to give you some information very quickly Mister Nikola and then go. The information is an alphanumeric sequence, maybe scrambled, but that is all I have at this time," TC told Nikola. He left a note and went back to his hotel. Before he went back he said why is it that your CDC does not realize that viruses actually *do* discriminate?

What was this alpha numeric sequence? How important and how urgent is it? They can't force him to provide more data as they may lose his cooperation. They can't torture the man…illegal here, but customary in Chima and with their allies. They do that to millions of people and the West can only object to it. Do they care or listen? Of course not.

The alphanumeric sequence was "c1tagpsfctehf10" and the relevant government agencies are put on notice to decode it. The FBI's computers get in action to find the closest words that contains the alpha numeric code provided by TC. They quickly come up with three human genes that contain these alphas, but what is that mysterious 10 again and why human genes? The CDC is alerted since TC had also talked about a vaccine.

Innocenti's appeal is coming up shortly. How will that go and is he going to be convicted?

Now we need to go back to our poor Innocenti. Was he on any video recording when he "committed" the crime? Hmmm, was he the killer? Yes, in the minds of Anna's family, but not until he is proven guilty of the crime in our own system of justice. Let's find out how Innocenti's trial goes.

His trial starts, and everything is stacking up against Innocenti. The Jurors are selected and the evidence for and against Innocenti will be presented. The 12 members of the Jury panel are about to hear both sides and review all evidences.

The prosecutor goes first and very briefly presented the State's case against Innocenti. The prosecutor thinks he has a slam-dunk case, thinking he can easily get him convicted.

Now it is time for the defense to present their case and evidence. Dwight Dershowitz turns to the Jurors and emphatically states.

"Ladies and gentlemen, I know you are twelve simple men and women of this country. You believe in justice, each one of you has a family, and you care for them. I ask each and every one of you to imagine this innocent man comes to you and asks you to stand up. He takes your seat, asks you to come down here and take his seat…right here, and now I am *your* attorney," Dershowitz says, as he firmly puts his finger on Innocenti's chair and raises his voice.

"You are now considered a murderer, but in your heart of hearts, and more importantly in your mind, you know that you have not committed this awful act of murder. Dear members of this important Jury…I am talking to you, please hear me out," Dershowitz gives the Jurors and the court a 10 second silence and while lowering his voice he continues. "You do not want to kill another innocent person to justify the killing of innocent Anna. Two wrongs won't make it right," Dershowitz tells the Jurors with passion, almost crying.

"Now, it is you against the power and resources of the State and Federal government leaning heavily on you. Don't forget that you are sitting *here*, not there. Now I am defending *you*. Their intent is to kill you, and that is all they want. How can you prove your innocence? Anyone…anyone, can have your blood and at some point may have had your skin and framed you by planting those at the murder scene. We have had the skin analyzed by experts. The chemicals and growth hormones found in the skin are not those of this innocent man. We engaged the best experts in the field and analyzed the DNA and skin tissues and the experts have testified to this fact. This man has recently had a brain surgery by a famous surgeon. He has a twin brother with the same DNA, and we know that his twin brother, Mr. Buzz Armstrong, could not have committed the crime because he was physically out in the Space Station," He continues.

"Ladies and gentlemen, this innocent man has not committed this murder. He knows that and all his God-loving supporters know that…the people of his church…many here, they can vouch for this man's integrity. We are sure that his blood and his skin have been planted at the murder scene to frame him, by someone. Not his brother, and not his brother's wife…her name has been cleared of all charges. But this man, this innocent man, he is not the murderer the government is looking for. Don't kill this innocent man," Dershowitz takes his case directly to the Jurors.

"I ask all of you ladies and gentlemen, the prosecutor's other so called proof was that this innocent man had gone to the scene of the murder that day. We know that and he does not deny that, but he did not go there to kill anyone. No, he is not capable of doing that. He went there to meet Ms. Amy D. Fragrant to discuss his brother's unfortunate 'alleged' affair with her. We have asked Ms. Fragrant to come and testify as to the substance of her meeting with this innocent man. We have no doubt that the killer who had planted the blood and skin will be found. He or she is somewhere, probably listening to us and laughing at all of us right now. But I ask you ladies and gentlemen… can you live a happy conscious life if you convict and kill this man, and then the killer comes forward, or is found? Can you imagine carrying this heavy unbearable burden on your shoulders and in your mind for the rest of your lives? You won't be able to bring him back to life, will you?"

Next the prosecutor presents a counter argument.

"Ladies and gentlemen, don't forget that the capable attorney of this murderer is giving you a bunch of what if's and not facts. He tells you 'if' the real murderer is found, but I tell you, there is no what if. No other murderer will be found. The killer of Anna is sitting right here in this chair. His attorney told you what 'if' the murderer is listening to us. There is no what if. He is listening to us. He is present here, sitting in this chair. This man, Innocenti Cristo, is the murderer. He premeditated the well-planned murder. He executed the killing! His blood and skin have been found there at the scene of the murder. He was there in that city far away from home, why? He comes up with a fabricated story about an affair…actually maybe it was his own affair he is talking about. He left his cell phone at the church hours away to cheat on his wife and not be tracked. He got gas in his city so that he is not seen in any gas station, and he even got extra gas in a gas can. Who in the world can come up with such a well-planned murder but this man…this murderer sitting right here? I only ask you not to be fooled by his well-dressed and talkative attorney," The prosecutor slams his hands on the table with passion and anger as he finishes his statement.

The Judge asked if Dershowitz has any counter comments, and he passes for now. They had previously in another session provided the DNA records and the analysis of experts went through it for the Jurors to be informed. Now it is the prosecutor's turn again and he calls this witness, Mrs. Amy Fragrant, to testify.

This woman who is testifying had blue hair like those of young stars, with heavy makeup, neon lipstick, tight leathery pants molded to her tall sexy-looking legs. Can anyone believe this witness with her looks? Is this woman the same woman who wanted to confess and repent? She looked and behaved with her sexy voice like a lady who was just ready to date and meet new guys. She didn't look like a woman who had cleaned up her act, but the prosecutor had no choice but to put her on the stand. She looked like a practiced con artist, chewing her gum, but there was no choice but to question her. She is now being sworn in, let's listen.

"Mrs. Fragrant, would you please come up here and be sworn in and sit here? And please honor our court, no chewing gum here," The Judge says.

"Yes, your honor," Amy apologized and was sworn in.

"Mrs. Fragrant, have you ever lied in your life?" the Prosecutor asked.

"Well, yes of course, haven't *you*?" Amy replied.

"Ma'am, we are talking about your honesty and how it affects this case and not mine. I am not on trial here, this murderer is. And I ask you to please give an answer to the question asked," The Prosecutor told Mrs. Fragrant.

"Yes sir," she answered flatly.

"Thank you. Are you married?" The prosecutor asked.

"Yes sir," She answered again, in the same tone.

"You met with Mr. Cristo that day...this murderer, did you not? And what were you discussing that day with Mr. Cristo in that park?" He asks quickly.

"Yes, I met him in that park, and I was discussing my affair with his brother, Buzz, you know....the famous astronaut," Amy answered casually.

"And among so many people, why did you have to tell that to Mr. Cristo?" The Prosecutor inquires.

"Well, I was under pressure to tell someone in that family. I had seen Mr. Armstrong before, on TV of course. I follow the space missions and I had also seen Mr. Cristo...at his church...and I could easily guess that they were identical twins because of their exact same looks," Amy replied.

"I still don't see that as a good reason to disclose his brother's secret affair to Mr. Cristo, do you?" Questioned the prosecutor.

"Well, I did, but maybe I should not have...but then he is a man of God. I thought by confessing to him, who is the closest to God and close to Mr. Armstrong, that God himself may forgive me. Maybe I am a fool thinking that way, but I thought it was right," Mrs. Fragrant commented.

"No, I assure you, Mrs. Fragrant that you are not a fool, you are..." The prosecutor pauses for a few seconds and continues "you are a very smart woman. I only hope you are not..." The prosecutor changed his mind and did not finish his sentence, "but I really hope you are being truthful here," He finished.

"Yes I assure you of that and I have no reason to lie, no other government....., sorry no other person is forcing me to testify here...this has been very embarrassing to me and my husband. We may go through divorce as a result," Amy replied.

"But, Mrs. Fragrant, you also met with Mrs. Mary Armstrong, right? Why did you have to do that?...Were you trying to cause marital problems between them so that you may give your affair a bit more continuity? After all he is a famous astronaut, is he not?" The prosecutor asked with emphatic voice.

"No sir, my intention was to get it off of my chest, and let her know about it too. I ask you not to embarrass me anymore in this court," Amy answered and pleaded.

"Well, would you have liked it, Mrs. Fragrant, if Mrs. Armstrong called and met your husband to tell him about your secret affair?" The prosecutor asked, with a mocking tone.

"Would I have liked that? Well of course not, but if that satisfied her, it would have been her choice to make," Amy said with a thoughtful look upon her face.

"What time did you meet Mr. Cristo, and for how long?" Asked the Prosecutor sharply.

"I think it was late morning, and we talked about thirty minutes or so," Amy answered quickly.

"Was Mr. Cristo…I ask you Mrs. Fragrant…was Mr. Cristo in any kind of panic mode, nervous, or stressed out? In other words, did you see any abnormal behavior in his words or facial expressions?" The prosecutor asked.

"To be honest with you, yes…he did show some facial anxiety, but he told me his wife didn't know that he had gone there to meet me so maybe that was the reason for his stressed-out behavior. He was also carrying a device that had a small screen. The electronic device showed a fluctuating graph with variation on the screen and I asked him what it was. He said his brain surgeon had given it to him to monitor his aggression level. He was supposed to carry it for as long as he needed it. He told me that he was also prescribed a pill and if he ever felt his aggression was acting up he should hook up the device to his arm. Then if the device also confirms it he should quickly take two pills. Anyway, you could see the graph on the monitor was way up when I looked at it, but I am not a doctor, so I don't know. I do think the man is innocent though," Mrs. Fragrant replied.

"Mrs. Fragrant, please leave his defense to his good attorney. You don't need to defend this murderer," Said the Prosecutor hastily.

"Objections your honor, the prosecutor is trying to suppress this witness's testimony when it is not going his way. We need all the facts to come out. It is this man's life on the line," Dershowitz told the Judge.

"Over-ruled, you may continue Mrs. Fragrant," The Judge told the prosecutor to continue.

"Mrs. Fragrant, after you told him about your affairs with his brother, did he try to start the same type of relationship with you, just like you had with his brother…at least a quick one?" The Prosecutor said, getting close to her and talking slowly.

Amy turned her face to the Judge. She began screaming at him in outrage. "No sir, I did not...and he did not try to do that either. And I don't appreciate your line of suggestion. I was there to confess, and it was a mistake...may my God forgive me. I'm so embarrassed,"

The Judge looked at the officer in the court, as if to give him a hint for him to be ready in case this outraged woman were to attack the Judge or someone. The officer pulled his gun out in one hand and pepper spray in the other, to be ready, just in case.

"What kind of frigging Judge are you?" Mrs. Fragrant shouted.

"Why aren't you defending me? This man is accusing me as if I run around initiating sexual affairs with just anyone who comes in contact with me, damn it. What kind of ineffective Judge are you?"

The Judge raised his gavel and pointed it at her. With a loud and trembling voice he spoke to her. "Mrs. Fragrant, if you don't watch the way you talk I will throw your ass in jail for contempt of court. Ma'am do you understand me, or should I use any other language for you to understand? Chimese, German, Arabic? You can be thrown in jail for a few years," He began coughing badly. He was irate and felt provoked. The coughing continued, as if he had injured his vocal cords.

Amy waited for his cough to subside, looking down. "My apologies your honor,"

The officer relaxed and put his gun back in his holster.

The prosecutor and Mrs. Fragrant go through some other questions and answers, and then her questioning ends with, "Ok thank you, Mrs. Fragrant, I have no further questions,"

"Mr. Dershowitz, do you have any questions for Mrs. Fragrant?" The Judge asked.

"Yes your honor, just a couple of questions for her," Dwight said.

"Mrs. Fragrant when you met Mr. Cristo, were you wearing a pair of thin plastic gloves, the ones the surgeons use? We are also told that you offered him a couple of cut pieces of an apple. How did he cut his hand? Did it bleed? Was there a piece of skin that came off his finger? And how did you clean it off?" Dwight asked.

"I don't know what you are talking about. These are fabricated lies. What apple and what knife? I was asked if I ever lied, but you are lying through your teeth sir. None of these things happened, you liar," Amy said with a hot red face.

The Judge asked her to be more respectful.

"But Mrs. Fragrant this is not what we have heard from Mr. Cristo under oath. He has told us that you poked his finger, and after you cleaned it you took the tissue containing his skin and put them in a plastic bag and took it with you to dispose of it 'properly.' Has he lied to us under oath and did you use that word 'properly' regarding the disposal of the blood and skin? Mrs. Fragrant…did you kill Anna and put this innocent man's blood and skin at the murder scene to frame him?" Mr. Dershowitz asked peering directly into her eyes.

"Objections your honor. Mr. Dershowitz is accusing this innocent lady of a murder without any evidence," The prosecutor said.

The judge orders her to answer the question.

"You must be ashamed of yourself to make that suggestion. I am sure you can check his fingerprint on the knife," Suggested Mrs. Fragrant.

"Mrs. Fragrant a minute ago you told us that there was no knife and no apple…yet you just told us to check his fingerprint on the knife. Which one of your statements was a lie? You killed Anna, didn't you Mrs. Fragrant? I ask you again, did you kill Anna and spread this innocent man's blood on Anna's body? Please be truthful, as you are under oath," Dwight pressed.

"Oh, I misspoke…his story about any knife or apple is absolutely a lie," Amy said, trying to clarify her remarks.

"Mrs. Fragrant when you were asked a question by the prosecutor your answer was…and I'll quote you here…you said 'Yes I assure you of that, I have no reason to lie, no other government…..sorry no other person is forcing me to testify here.' Mrs. Fragrant, why did the word 'other government' unconsciously slipped out of your mouth and you immediately changed it to other persons? Mrs. Fragrant are you an agent of a foreign government? And I ask you again, did you kill Anna and spread this innocent man's blood on Anna's body?" Dwight asked as he pressed the questions harder.

All of a sudden Mrs. Fragrant starts crying. Is she buying time to prepare an answer? Is she the killer and will she admit to that? She asks to get some Kleenex tissues and finally talks after 2 minutes.

"Why do you accuse me of such treason? Can you prove that I worked for Chima?" She asked.

"No, Mrs. Fragrant, I didn't accuse you of working for Chima. But if you were not, then why did you pick Chima among many countries? I didn't mention that country myself. Any special relationship with them Mrs. Fragrant?" Dwight asked with a slight smile.

"No sir, and as I told you I do not work for any foreign government, and I repeat I did not kill Anna," Mrs. Fragrant stated, trying to sound calm and convincing.

"Thank you, Mrs. Fragrant. No other questions at this time your honor," Dwight said.

After the parties go through more questions and answers the defense and the prosecutor had no further questions. The Judge asked her to go down to the floor and up to her seat.

"Mrs. Fragrant, you may step down…and please be careful. These steps are a bit slippery…we had a serious accident here yesterday. We had to call in an ambulance when this poor older lady fell and broke her hip. We may hear from her attorney soon, and we should. You know when you are old and have a major bone cracked, even after surgery involving bones, you can have a heart attack or pulmonary embolism. That is how I lost my mom," The honest Judge said, causing a bit of laughter and sorrow from all sides. He wanted to sound like a doctor and forgot that he is only a Judge but tried to give good advice.

The court session ended and Innocenti's attorneys held several other meetings. They brought his brother Buzz to the court and asked him many questions and they also brought other character witnesses. They brought in the garbage collector, among others, who were all questioned.

After both the prosecutor and defense attorney rest their case, it is time for the Jurors to speak. The judge had already asked the Jurors to go over all relevant information and spend as much time as needed to render a verdict. After two days of deliberations, the Jury panel has made a unanimous decision. The Judge asks for the decision to be read.

"After reviewing all relevant facts and considering the honorable Judge's recommendation as to the relevance of the evidence presented and as our civil duty requires, we, the duly appointed Jurors, by our unanimous vote find Mr. Innocenti Cristo guilty of first-degree murder," The lead Juror states.

Sadness prevails and then a burst of cry. Innocenti is holding his head down as his wife is crying and Innocenti's parents are in absolute shock. Innocenti is taken into the State custody and then to jail.

Chapter 6

Charles

Now we talked about the life of Buzz and Innocenti, but I had promised to take you back to the beginning of our story when Scotty was delivering the babies. So let us go back and find out what happened after the first child was born. Another Quantum Jump, if you will…

"Push Marsha honey, the second one is almost out. Maybe a girl…we will know shortly sweetheart. Marsha…are you ok? Oh my God I think she is passing out. Oh my Lord, why is she not responding? Come on hun," Scotty urges and gives her a bit of a shake and checks her breathing.

Scotty brings the second child out, but now notices a leg of the third child was also out. He is shocked they have triplets and not twins. Marsha does not know it and Scotty is wondering what he is supposed to do. He is now just panicking and thinking to himself. Marsha had taught him previously that the baby's head must come out first, so he carefully turns the baby's body and pulls him out.

Unfortunately, the third one is born lifeless, not breathing. How can he tell this to Marsha, and especially when we are not even sure if Marsha herself is still alive? Charles quickly cuts the umbilical cord and tries to resuscitate Marsha a few times, but she is not responding. He takes the third child to the barn and quickly gives him CPR, only just a few times with no luck and quickly rushes back to the other babies and Marsha.

Marsha is not dead and has just gained consciousness, "Scotty where were you, where did you go?" Marsha asked, talking so slowly with a fainted voice.

"Oh, nowhere…I ran out and sneezed. I did not want the kids with weak immune systems to get exposed, not on their first day of their lives," Scotty replied.

"But I was looking through the window as I was lying on the bed…and I think I saw you coming from the barn. I think I had passed out…maybe I became delusional," Marsha said, weakly.

"Honeybun, my love, it is all done…be happy and look at your two beautiful innocent sons. They are all born. They look so healthy and you are ok too. You had passed out before the third…," Scotty began.

Before Scotty could finish his sentence, Marsha screamed. "Did we have triplets?" Marsha asked with a worried look, but anxious to know.

"Oh no, no…my tongue slipped…I meant to say birth, but I said third. You are not alone, see honey. You are not the only one stressed out…I am too," Scotty said.

"I love you Scotty, but you know we can hardly maintain the twins, we just could not have handled three…no way," She commented.

Since Marsha had heard the word 'third' coming out of Scotty's mouth, she was scared that maybe there were triplets and one was born dead and Scotty did not want her to know. She thought the sneezing story was a fake, so she confronted Scotty again.

"Scotty, did we have triplets and one was born dead? Is that why you went to the barn and the sneezing story was a fake? You just wanted to cover it up, didn't you? Just tell me if that was the case," Marsha said.

"Oh no absolutely not. I assure you all were born healthy," Scotty said, trying to sound reassuring to Marsha.

In an hour or so Scotty goes back to the barn to see what needs to be done with the unfortunate case of the third baby, but suddenly hears a baby sound. The baby had not died and is alive, so what is he going to do now. He is shocked but happy, does not tell this to Marsha but attends to the baby for a day or two. It was extremely hard to hide the baby from Marsha, but she was not coming out of the cabin and just staying in to regain her weight and energy back. He was exchanging the three babies for a couple of days without Marsha noticing it, so they all got enough mother's milk.

Scotty and Marsha were constantly arguing whether they should let the babies be adopted by others. At some point they had even talked about abortion before the babies were born. They finally had concluded that it was best for the babies to be adopted.

"Scotty, you know we have been talking about the twins and I agree with you that it is in the best interest of these two little innocent babies to be raised in a family who can provide for them. We just cannot raise them here in a responsible way unless we move back down to the city. We just can't do it...no money...we can hardly survive. We don't want the kids to know they were adopted, so how are we going to do that?" Marsha asked.

"Well, we can give them to two different families or just leave them in the small-town church without them knowing," Scotty replied.

"Ok, do you think we can try to raise at least one of them?" Marsha asked.

"Well, we can try that honey, but I think we should go ahead and let both be adopted. We may become so attached to the one, it will be much harder to do it then, and it won't be fair to the other," Scotty said.

Scotty and Marsha finally decided to go ahead with the adoption, but not going through the awfully long official adoption process, and just by giving away the children to other families.

So next day, early in the morning he told Marsha that he has to take the old truck to a mechanic shop down in the city. His plan is, without Marsha's knowledge, to take the third child, the one Marsha did not know about, and to leave him at someone's doorstep. So, he puts the child in a wooden box bedded with some straw and a small blanket and started the long trip downhill.

On the way a policeman stops him.

'Where are you going, my friend?" The officer asked.

"Going to the mechanic shop to get my car fixed," Scotty answered.

The officer heard a baby's sound and suspects something is out of ordinary. Then he becomes very suspicious when he sees Scotty acting a bit nervously.

"What was that sound?" The officer asked.

"It is my baby... err, I meant my baby cat in the car," Scotty replied.

"A baby cat?" The officer gave him a strange look and was still suspicious. "Oh, ok sir. I will follow you to the mechanic shop," he said, in a friendly tone.

"Oh, my goodness what do I tell him if he sees the child?" Scotty is thinking. So, they stop at the mechanic shop and the officer goes to the car and opens the back door, but suddenly the officer's cell phone rings.

"Hello," The officer answers his cell phone.

"Hey man, where in the hell are you, stupid, careless man! Come back home right now! I have cut my finger off and it's just hanging by a thin skin. They will have to reattach it quickly and we need to go to the hospital. Get here now," The officer's wife said, in a panic.

The officer takes off so quickly and leaves Scotty and drives away.

"Thank you Lord," Scotty is thinking as he says hello to the mechanic shop owner and tells him he just stopped by to say hi.

Scotty continues going around and finally spots a suitable house. He gives a kiss to his baby and leaves him by the doorstep as he knocks on the door a few times and runs away to watch from behind a big tree. He waits about five minutes and finally the door opens. A woman screams as she sees a baby at her doorstep. He remembers where the house was "Number 101, Main Street".

Scotty rushes out without being noticed. We are now back in the mountain cabin.

"So, what did the mechanic say?" Marsha asked.

"Oh nothing…there were no problems with the car. The rattling stopped on the way down there," Scotty replied.

The third child grew up in this family. They were not kind people and arguing all the time. A mean couple causing conflicts and constantly using foul language as if it were the order of everyday. This was not a nice environment for a child to grow in, but who knows, maybe all these conflicts formed the child's brain to become a very peace-loving person.

The following day he puts one of the newborns in a wooden box early in the morning and went to a different local town on the east side of the mountain. He left the child in a very tiny local church's doorstep and watched from faraway to make sure the baby was taken in by a random God-loving church goer.

"Honey, I left the baby in the city's local church. I am sure he will be in better hands of caring people and they can raise him better and give him a good education," Scotty said.

This little baby turned out to be our Buzz Armstrong, the proud astronaut.

Another day passes, Scotty puts the second child in a safe big plastic basket and goes to a very slow-moving river passing through the small town. He notices some people sitting by the riverbank talking, painting and enjoying the day. He leaves the baby on the slow-moving water, close to the bank. He goes next to a couple and points to the container and says, "Oh my god, what in the world is in that basket…it looks like there is a baby in it," He wanted to get the attention of the couple. The woman screams and asks her husband to go get the basket, so he does. Scotty quietly goes back to his car and drives away.

Scotty wanted to get involved with the child that Marsha did not know about. Scotty knew in which house's doorstep he had left him, "101 Main Street." He lost track of the other two kids, but somehow had a desire to see how this third child, whom he had hidden in the barn, was growing up. He somehow had more connection with him.

One late morning he goes down to the city and knocks on the door of the house. "Who is it?" The resident asks and opens the door.

"Oh hi, I am so sorry to have bothered you sir, but I don't have a computer to print a flyer. I thought I'd just stop by and see if you want your house painted. I am a handy man…I can fix cars and do many other handymen works as well. You see, my wife and I live on the mountain top here and since I have no overhead I can do my work for cheap," Scotty explained. "I come here to buy groceries and stuff, and any time you want me I can work for you sir,"

The man had a very rough-looking, tanned face. He asked Scotty how much he would charge for the exterior of this big house to be painted and to make sure he gets the job, Scotty gave him a low price of $400, provided the owner paid for the paint. The man already had another quote of $2,500 so the stingy man jumped on Scotty's offer.

"When can you start?" He asked.

"I can start today sir," Scotty said.

So, they agreed for him to start the job and he goes back to the mountain cabin and tells Marsha that he can start doing some handy work for people and make some money. This, of course was an excuse to get to see the child more often. Scotty's plan worked and he got to see the boy growing up. This child got closer and closer to Scotty, almost like a stepdad and began confiding in Scotty on various subjects.

Some fifteen years passed, and this kid, named Charles, is now a trouble-maker, smart and naughty. In this household, you had to be a naughty boy to survive. Surprisingly, he was also extremely kind. Strange and incompatible traits for a boy to have. He always talked with his adoptive parents about humanity in general and the biological problems that human species have.

One morning on their mountain top cabin, Scotty notices a fire down somewhere in the small town.

"Marsha, come here quickly! Look at the town, down there. There is some kind of fire going on. You want to go see it with me? I'm so curious," Scotty said as he was grabbing his shoes.

As they were getting closer and closer to the city Scotty tells Marsha, "I hope it is not the house that I have been doing some handy work on. I know the owners and their son, Charles…a little devil…but he kind of likes me. I also did some electrical work for them last month or so," Scotty finished.

As they were getting closer to the area where the fire was, the location of the smoke seemed to be near to the house Charles was living in.

"Oh gosh, it *is* their house on fire! Let me go help!" Scotty screams and jumps out of the car to quickly rush to help. The owner of the house and his wife are screaming and don't know what to do. He sees Scotty and cries, "Scotty, please help! Please, please!"

"What is going on?" Scotty cries back. "Where is Charles?"

"Oh God, Charles went in to get our cat, but he is not out yet. The firefighters are here now getting their stuff ready," Dick said.

Scotty felt that Charles is stuck somewhere so he rushes in. The firefighters try to stop him, but there was no stopping. Scotty knows that it is his son who is in trouble and thinks as he runs, 'why did we let this boy be adopted? His fate would have been so different. Maybe better.' Scotty was blaming himself but searching frantically.

"Charles, Charles, where are you?" Scotty screams. He continues calling for Charles, searching different rooms full of smoke…he himself is in danger of suffocating. 'Oh my god, it is so hot and smoky here, I need to go out.' "I have to find my son! Hey Charles, my dear son…where are you, where are you?" Scotty is screaming and now his own pants and sleeves are on fire.

Scotty sees Charles holding a cat, his clothes on fire, running and burning. Scotty takes Charles in his arms and comes out of the house. He puts out the fire on Charles' clothes, but Charles is charred…his face is in bad shape. You could not even recognize him; it is that bad. The firefighters continue to put out the fire. Scotty himself is also severely burned.

The paramedics arrive in an ambulance and transported Charles, with his parents to the hospital. Scotty and Marsha followed them to the hospital's emergency room. Fortunately, this hospital had a multidisciplinary team that had worked on burn victims, but the severity of the burn was so much that Charles had already gone into a coma. The doctors with the burn team had to concentrate on saving his life first and not so much worry about his looks.

Scotty also got some burns as he was carrying Charles putting out fires on Charles' clothing. The doctor approached the parents. Is Charles dead, Does the doctor have any bad news?

"Are you the parents?" The doctor asks.

"Yes Doctor, I am Dick Alvin, Charles' father…and this is my wife Carolyn," Mr. Alvin says.

"Hello Carolyn, I am Doctor Gupta," They all greet each other as Dr. Gupta continues. "I don't have good news," Dr. Gupta says.

Charles' mother screams, "Is my son gone, oh my God!"

"Oh no, he is still alive but Charles' burns are extremely severe, my team is working on him. The burn is all over his body and I have to be upfront with you…we have to do our best to save his life first…chances are ok but not great…but we will do our best," Dr. Gupta tells the parents.

"Thank you, Doc. I know you and your team will do the utmost. Thanks again," Dick commented.

The doctors were concerned about infection, breathing issues, joint fracture impairment, scarring and other factors that can affect his survival and his overall functionality and looks. All of these factors can affect, delay, and complicate the healing process. Dick thanked Scotty for trying to save Charles' life. Scotty also got some medical attention as well for his burns.

"He would have been dead had it not been for you going in our burning house to bring him out," Dick told Scotty.

"Oh no, my duty Dick, I felt like I was saving my own son, I have so much passion for him," Scotty replied with tear in his eyes. After some time and talking to Dick and Carolyn, they went back to their cabin. Scotty starts talking to Marsha.

"Sweetheart, you know how much I love you, don't you?" Scotty asks Marsha.

"Of course. I think you have something to tell me. What is it…tell me," Marsha pleads.

"Well, Charles is our own child. We had triplets and I had not told you that when you delivered the babies," Scotty confesses.

"Oh my God, why didn't you tell me that? Why did you hide it from me? I am shocked! So you lied to me…why, why?" Marsha asked with a bit of anger.

"I don't know…he was born dead. I was scared…I was so nervous. I didn't know what I was doing I guess. I just could not give you the news, so I took his dead body to the barn and tried to resuscitate him quickly without much luck and I came back to see if you were ok. Then I never told you that in a few hours when I went to bury the child he had come alive. I quickly thought if I could hide him that I could just let him be adopted. I don't know honey, now I think maybe I was crazy…insane…stupid. And as a result this little boy is now burned," Scotty cries, in tears and confessing his mistake to his one and only love.

Scotty and Marsha go back and forth to the hospital almost daily seeing Dick and Carolyn at Charles' bedside and talked to them. After four days Charles is still in a coma. The family stands by his bed and continually prays. Well, Charles survives and comes out of his coma, but has been burned so severely that his face looks bad and unrecognizably deformed. For sure he will need some facial reconstructive surgeries.

After a couple of weeks of agony, but with so much care at the hospital, the doctors gather and discuss how to give Charles new skin. Dr. Gupta and others do not see any good unaffected section of the body for skin grafts. They also did not want an additional burden on his body, taking the good skin off one place for facial reconstruction and needing additional healing. The doctor asks the father if he is a good match and is willing to give a skin graft to Charles.

"Dr. Gupta, I would love to do that, but I have to be honest with you, Carolyn and I adopted Charles. But go ahead test my blood. Who knows… maybe I will be a good match. But furthermore Doctor, we both have hepatitis B, so we may not be good candidates to start with," Dick told Dr. Gupta.

"Oh, God bless you for doing that. No problem, we can get it from our skin bank. You both need to take care of your hepatitis, you know. I will talk to you both later," Dr. Gupta told the parents.

Scotty jumps to the discussion. "Oh Doctor, if you want I am also willing to get my blood tested for a match,"

"Don't worry sir, we will have him taken care of. Because of the severity of the burn we will need a split-thickness skin graft. This causes less rejection by the immune system. I don't think we need composite graft, at least not now, but we may need full thickness graft for some areas," Dr. Gupta explained.

Marsha, now knowing that Charles is her own child, also volunteers, but Dr. Gupta rejects her offer.

Charles gets various kinds of skin grafts as needed and continues with his life. This smart boy goes to a famous university, studies biology and medicine, gets a second degree in electrical engineering and becomes a brain surgeon. He studies chemistry as a minor in college and is incredibly talented in all fields. He loves making miniatured gadgetry of all kinds. This naughty, loving, curious boy is now the talk of the academia and the society of brain surgeons. At the age of 28 Charles becomes the most famous brain surgeon, biologist, virologist and epidemiologist in the country…possibly in the world. He started collaborating with his Chimese counterpart and their famous biology labs and Chima CDC.

Charles had worked for a few famous biotech companies before he started his own sophisticated and very advanced bio lab. Later on he opened his own brain surgery center, invested in the latest operating room equipment, the latest MRI and X-ray machines, electron microscopes, and other major gene sequencing machines, with the fastest computing systems available anywhere in the world. He used Quantum Computers for many applications to increase the security of the lab data. He had become so famous that many medical equipment manufacturers were begging him to have them make specialty machines just for his lab and surgery center. His lab is now the largest in the country.

His main specialty, other than virology and gene sequencing, was being the most famous in the world for developing brain tissues outside of the brain. In his lab he worked on implanting tissues into the brain, creating specific behavioral patterns in his patients and easily manipulating the long axons going through the Corpus Callosum pathways, connecting or redirecting the two sides of the brain. Chima had become so interested in learning from Charles and potentially using his very sophisticated and advanced bio lab.

Dealing with Chima however may become dangerous.

Charles had established the most advanced security system at his lab. He had selected reputable companies in the country to implement security measures. They had covered biosafety, protecting microbial agents and toxins, pathogenic organisms, biological terrorism, accountability for specimen, threat assessments and data transfer using their quantum computers. Charles, for obvious reasons, was concerned about Chima's espionage stealing his unique genetic engineering technology.

Charles had an awfully close relationship with his workmate, Tycho Atomos, with almost no work secret between them. So, let's Quantum Jump and listen in as he is discussing various subjects with Tycho.

"You know Tycho, because of my travel back and forth to Chima and my credible connections I can't be specific in what I am going to tell you, but I am a bit concerned. Without going into much detail I will only give you a hint. What if our country developed an extremely fast Ultra-Wideband wireless network and used it only for military use without anyone or any other country knowing about it? You know other countries sometimes are so much ahead of us, but with more evil goals. And I am not talking about the slow 5G network," Charles continued.

"Tycho, unfortunately as a country we make major policy and military directional changes every four or eight years, but other countries have 40 year plans. They keep their military and bioweapons really secret and that can bring an end to their adversaries...a sudden death. I am not a military man... only a biologist, and more importantly an epidemiologist. I can't be more specific, so let's change the subject now before I get into trouble and please...this is just between the two of us," Charles told Tycho.

"I know that makes me nervous too...Chima's aggressive military operations and bio labs are advanced, but they also need our company's bio lab data and input in so many different ways. Without us...I mean without you and your knowledge...they are dead in the water. You are the most famous biologist. Your knowledge on genetic engineering and gene sequencing techniques and the tools that you have developed manipulating viruses and bacteria are unmatched. Much more advanced than theirs...faster and more efficient than CRISPR technology that they are using. Your methods are much more precise. Are you worried about any military danger when it comes to Chima and Rubbas or worried about any bio wars?" Tycho asked, trying to get more specifics from Charles.

"Well, maybe all. My worries are not on any kind of military attack. Military attacks are extremely useless and counterproductive compared to bioweapons, especially if the bio attack is coupled with military equipment, satellites and other architectures. We appreciate having 5G available to everyone but imagine what much higher generations will do. Keep in mind, I am not saying they have that," Charles explained.

"Ok, so why and what are you worried about the most?" Tycho asked.

"It is the speed that excites me, but also concerns me the most. Imagine if generation 5G has the speed of 5 to 10 Gigabytes per second. What would much higher speed be like? Now combine that with a latency, or the delay of the signal packs from one node to another of less than 1 millisecond versus 300 millisecond of generation 5…and further combine that with the use of Cloud Radio Access Network for better efficiency and you got a complete system for military to overcome any adversary's system. The end can come in hours, not days. When another country has everything in cloud, ubiquitous computing and remote access and real time control of computers…and most importantly satellites, combined with…imbedded with software and human agents, placed where they need to be…it gives them power hard to overcome. That is all I can say," Charles concluded his remarks.

Having become proficient in the biomedical engineering field, Charles is now thinking about expanding his implantable and extremely small micro device and real human neuronal network created outside of ones' brain in a new and totally different experiment. With his vast experience in creating tiny gadgets, he is now ready to put it all in action, but who will be his prize winner or his victim? A man, a woman? For sure not animals anymore as he has already tested his micro devices on animals closest to humans. He confides in Tycho again.

"Tycho, I have to give you another secret," Charles said.

"Is it about Chima?" Tycho asked.

"Oh no, it is more personal. We were triplets when we were born, so I have two brothers who were also adopted. My real father, who let me be adopted, confided this fact with me, but made me promise that I will not try to find the other two to let them know about this. He didn't want the life of the children to be shaken. He wanted them to have their lives continued on their normal course with their adoptive parents. We were born in our own cabin house on the mountaintop with no doctor or even a nurse around," Charles continued.

"One of them is named Innocenti and I noticed he has made an appointment to see me. He had indicated that he has been told by his doctor that he has a meningioma tumor and he thinks I am a good candidate to perform his surgery. We require the patient to provide us with their picture and I could see the resemblance with my old look. Mistakenly he uploaded his picture when he was 15 years old to my secretary and then his new and latest picture was loaded. I am 100% positive that he is my brother," Charles said.

So finally, Charles and Innocenti meet and have a very medical type discussion and after Charles reviews his new MRI and X-Rays, his team makes a three-dimensional image of the tumor. He orders Innocenti to schedule an appointment for a surgery to take the tumor out. The surgery will take some 10 hours, Innocenti was told. Charles is shocked to see Innocenti's looks but Innocenti can only see a deformed burnt face of a surgeon.

He now has his prize winner selected...his own brother. His plan is to imbed his micro-miniature device and some neuronal network that he had developed in his lab. He had also developed a new drug to prohibit rejection of the new neurons that he was planning to imbed in Innocenti's brain. He wanted to see if all of this will work and how he can stop any seizures in the future and improve his potential aggression. He was sure that this system will not fail. Innocenti had indicated that he had a couple of seizures in the past and was worried about his aggressive mood changes. But will it work and calm Innocenti, or will it make him aggressive...making him capable of killing another person?

Charles had used *in vivo* functional imaging to create tens of thousands of interconnected neural circuits. His approach included calcium imaging with fluorescent signals to monitor neuron to neuron action, potential to find emergent properties of different magnitude. He had noticed that emergent properties suddenly show up when hundreds or thousands of neurons were connected. The same emergent properties, that is the marker of what we call consciousness at a larger level, a sudden creation of a mental state.

Charles had created many different types of brain modules and neural circuits using artificial intelligence after having one thousand computers fight in simulations with each other. Using the latest Artificial Intelligence software and deep brain simulation, he helped to create a module that if used in someone's brain that would suppress and almost eliminate aggression. He had used 2,000 micro electrodes connected to the brain. He used an fMRI machine on people with aggressive behavior and had identified what portion of the brain was becoming active when one shows aggression. He was planning to remove and replace tiny parts of some neuronal network during the operation. No lab in the world had done this type of analysis using 1,000 micro electrodes at a time. His plan was to have the same type of electrode placement on Innocenti during the operation to locate the exact neurotic tracts.

Later, we may Quantum Jump and read a few pages of Charles' books. One on gene sequencing and the other about philosophy of life and human aggression. The day has come and Innocenti is on the operating room talking to Charles and looking so innocent and a bit scared, as if he were not sure of coming back from anesthesia. He asks for forgiveness from his God and tells Charles to let his wife know how much he loves her. Maria and Innocenti's parents are waiting for the surgery to be done with.

During the surgery Charles carefully monitored and located a few neuronal networks inside Innocenti's brain that were the cause of his seizure, and very delicately replaced them with his developed neural circuits. At the end of the surgery he inserted a micro-miniature device as the operating room nurse notices and ask Charles, "What is that little device Doc?"

"Oh, it is to find out if there is any tumor growth without opening his brain again., it also monitors his aggression level. That way, we won't need to take any X-rays, which is not healthy, or perform any unnecessary MRIs. It is my latest innovation, an indicator of cancerous cell growth. We will take the device out in four years. This device I am putting in his brain will detect any protein markers on cancerous cells. It is for detecting Glioblastoma, which is an aggressive type of cancer. I am not worried about his meningioma. I may send him for proton radiation to kill a bit of the tumor I have to leave in his brain. As you saw, the tumor was so close to his central vein. I could have killed the man had I made a mistake cutting the vein," Charles told the nurse in the operating room.

Charles did notice a strange thing during the insertion of the device. A very tiny microchip attached to it had a different color. It was a light orange color instead of dark orange. He thought that maybe the color had faded due to it being around and exposed to chemicals in the lab. He was sure that no one else knew about this device other than his Chimese engineering counterpart Zin, who had brought the part to the operating room. Was it the same device or was a microchip in it replaced? Charles started thinking about it and started doubting.

Charles told the operating room nurses that Innocenti will be given another device to carry with him. The device among many other things will continuously record the level of Innocenti's aggression and potential seizure. Chance of seizure goes up if the tumor grows much larger, pressing on the other parts of the brain. He was also given some pills to take in case he notices his aggression has acted up significantly.

The brain surgery is finished, Charles informs Maria and the parents of Innocenti, who were happy and relieved. They go to see Innocenti, who was kept overnight and sent to rehab for a week to improve his walking and talking. His motor neurons were affected a bit as Charles pushed to release the tumor from the neighboring neurons.

Charles had another extremely close Chimese workmate friend, Chen G. Zhang. With Tycho, Charles shared data about innovations, but with his Chimese friend Chen, counterpart biologist, he worked very closely when it came to virology, vaccinations and especially epidemiology and the worldwide danger of a Pandemic.

In his heart of hearts Chen wanted to be an activist against Chima's People's Republican Army and communism. He was like the Gorbachev of the old Soviet Union who wanted to make drastic social and economic changes. He starts confiding in Charles.

Chen talked to Charles about Chima's history telling him that Chimese people are still distressed remembering their downfall from world power due to the opium wars of 1940s. They won't forget the formation of the Chinese Communist Party in 1921 that resulted in all of their suffering, murder and torture. After being the ruler of the world for centuries Chima wants to resurrect their nation and to rule the world again. Chen bases his remarks on the very evident Chinese leaders' comments, direct quotes and their national anthem. They must feed 1.3 billion people, but come to think of it so does India. So why Chima? Are they mean people? Chen does not think Chinese people are, but the communist party most probably is, he tells Charles.

Chen tells Charles that if Chima wanted to use bioweapons, it can also kill millions of their own people. Viruses don't discriminate…or do they? Of course, they do, he tells him…and this is exactly what Chima will use against the West. At least that is what their plan is. Viruses actually *do* discriminate. Viruses affect more people with different blood types, and they discriminate with people whose immune system is weakened, with asthma, or whose nutrient intake is not good. Most importantly, they will discriminate if they are not vaccinated. For Chima this was the key…vaccination. It does not matter what type of viruses. Chima will use this discriminatory behavior of the viruses against the U.S., since their population will not be vaccinated.

After millions of years of evolution and mutations the viruses know how to survive even though they are not "alive." That includes retroviruses, which are viruses that are composed not of DNA, but of RNA.

To accomplish their evil goal, Chima had previously realized how badly they needed Charles' help for some genetic sequencing and somehow they wanted him to have the ability to push him with threats or with a carrot stick if he did not cooperate. Will money do the job, or will they try other options first? Yes of course. They have plenty of money.

Chen was very trusted by the Chimese Communist Party and had been given the overall responsibility of overseeing their operation of their Center for Disease Control and Prevention, as it is called Chima CDC.

Chen had seen firsthand a systematic crackdown and violation of human rights and unfair trials and torture in internment camps. He had seen the secrecy of Chimese Communist Party on the use of the death penalty and repression. He knew about the communist party's statistics on prisoners and internment camps and child labor affecting millions of minority groups in Chima. Slavery? You decide.

Chima had already known the extent of Charles' knowledge and capability of his extremely large and advanced bio lab specializing in sequencing of genes, viruses, bacteria, and especially his better than CRISPR technology. Chima knew that Charles' lab is very advanced and had analyzed many major components. The antigens and others used in vaccine production, including adjuvants, antibiotics, stabilizers, preservatives, trace components and diluents. Chima desperately needed access to all of these to accomplish their mission. But what exactly is their mission? An evil mission? We will see, but for them speed was of utmost importance, and they have had this plan cooking for a long time.

The western labs learned so much from bacteria and how they dismantle viruses, now Chima can steal them for free.

Chapter 7
Elon

A couple of weeks back Charles was invited as a keynote speaker to a major International conference in Miami on "Genetic Engineering and Worldwide Pandemic." Over 2,500 famous biologists were present. After the conference was finished and Charles signed his books for many attendees, he came out of the conference, got into his car and started driving to come out of the parking. Suddenly, this boy of about fourteen years old jumped in front of his car. He almost hit the boy but managed not to. Charles came out to see if the boy was ok. He appeared to be.

"You could have been hurt badly," Charles said. "Why did you do that? What is your name?"

"I am Elon," The boy says. "I am sorry...I did not mean to scare you, but I needed to talk to you," Elon said.

"Oh, why Elon, why did you want to talk to me dear?" Charles asked.

"Somehow I had to see you. You are my hero and Icon," Elon said. "From the age of five I have always wanted to learn biology of life. I have studied a lot. I know about you and I have read all your articles and books. I am a Foster child living with my Foster parents," The boy tells him.

"Oh, that is good. So what happened to your parents, Elon?" Charles asked, and noticed a few tears dripping from the boy's eyes down to his cheeks. "Why are you crying, Elon?" Charles asked.

"I lost both my parents when our house caught on fire last year," Elon said.

"Sorry to hear that. You are a strong boy though...no need to cry. And we almost have had the same life experience. When I was fifteen years old our house caught on fire also. You can still see the result of the fire on my face, but we are both strong. You still haven't told me why you jumped in front of my car Elon," Charles tells him.

"I just turned fifteen today and I know much about biology. I know I could never be allowed to come to your conference, but I had heard you were here, so I took my chances. This was my only way to force you to see me," Elon replied, and confidently added, "I know so much that I think I know more about biology than you do. And I hope this does not offend you,"

"Well, happy birthday, and no you have not offended me at all. I am glad that you know more than I do. I always want to learn more, so maybe I can arrange for you to teach me," Charles said, enjoying the confidence this boy showed at this young age. "Let me call your foster parents and let them know you are with me. I will of course introduce myself, and if they allow us I will take you back to the conference theater and show you all the videos and slides showing the latest. Would you like that?" Charles asked.

"Oh, I would love it," Elon replied.

So, Charles called Elon's foster parents, who knew who Charles was. He and Elon went back to see the videos and slides. It appeared that this boy was current on all new advances in biology and pandemics.

"Tell me Elon, did you like the whole thing?" Charles asked.

"I loved it! It was a good cursory review…piece of cake," Elon replied.

"Ok, now that you know so much, I will arrange for you to teach me everything…even the latest innovations," Charles said.

"I can confidently say that I know about biology, of course in theory, more than everyone in that conference," Elon said.

"That is great Elon! I know at my age I am still learning, and I felt humbled in front of all those famous scientists. Are you happy where you are with your foster parents?" Charles asked.

"Not really, and I hope that one day I will be adopted," Elon said. He paused and then looked thoughtfully up at Charles. "Hey, Mr. Charles, can I challenge you with a biology question sir?"

"You sure can, but you already know how much my level of knowledge is…maybe not much. Since you have read all my articles and books maybe I can test *your* knowledge a bit. By the way, there is no Mister or sir here, just call me Charles, ok?" Charles told Elon.

"You can ask me anything, I am ready," Elon said.

"Ok Elon, what do the words 'software and apple' remind you of in terms of biology? Charles questions.

"Well, I can write a few books about them. Anything specific you want me to talk about?" Elon asks.

"No, whatever comes to your mind," Charles states.

"Well let's say as we rushed to type 'apple' we misspelled it. We use the find function of the software to locate the misspelled apple," Elon said and continued. "Imagine if we had the same capability in finding our genetic defect or trying to find a cure. Well, we have that…it is CRISPR, a genome-based technology," Elon said.

"Good Elon, and how did we acquire that knowledge?" Charles asked.

"Well the prokaryotes…let's say E-coli…have given us that capability. We learned from the bacteria's immune system it is called CRISPR/Cas9. For millions of years bacteria have been using that to fight viruses by chopping off a piece of the viral DNA. There is a constant bio war in us," Elon was on a roll and continued

"It is a powerful gene editing tool…disruptive innovation. It has two parts…two components…a DNA cutting protein called Cas9 that locates and binds to a common sequence called PAM, and then an RNA molecule called guide RNA that unwinds part of the double helix. Cas9 cuts it and we can insert the new sequence that we want. We can use CRISPR to correct it but if we are not careful we can mess up our DNA. The combination of the two results in a cut and paste tool for DNA editing. With this tool, we can cure many genetic diseases, such as Sickle cell disease among many others," Elon explained so confidently and continued, impressing Charles, who was already impressed.

"The problem is the find button finds only the letter you tell it to find. If each gene were producing only one protein, the job of genetic engineering and finding diseases would be easy…a piece of cake. But sometimes two, three or more genes need to cooperate. One addition or deletion in a gene or two can have drastic adverse effects on the body. Changes in genes can make you susceptible to getting a disease. Using this technology, we can knock out part of a gene or add a sequence into the genome or a gene," Elon finally finished.

Elon was so happy that Charles is really impressed. You could see it on his happy face.

"You know Charles, I only know these in theory. I only have a small microscope. I wish I could work in a lab. I could do wonders. I know how cells differentiate to make our different type of cells. I could even make a whole new human by reversing cells to 'de-differentiation' taking it back to zygote, I can," Elon stated proudly.

"That is great, but don't you think we still have some way to go to create a totally new person from our existing one?" Charles asked.

"Yeah, but I know how to reverse our biological time and reprogram skin cells back to its embryonic state or iPS cells of the same person. All I need is a lab," Elon says.

"Oh great, so if I let you use my lab and give you a piece of my skin you can make some brain cells and make Charles a smarter Charles? I am sure I can use a better, smarter brain; don't you think?" Charles inquires.

"No, you are as smart as I am, but maybe one day I can use a skin cell and take it even back to sperm and egg and implant it to produce a new person or human parts outside of the body. I can do that, believe me I can. Do you want me to talk about Cas/10 or Cas/13 or as you have jokingly said in your book Cas/1001?" Elon asked.

It was getting really late so Charles offered a gift to Elon, saying, "Let me sign my book for you with a special note. Would you like that?"

"I would love it...please do," Answered Elon.

Charles took one of his books and signed it and gave it to Elon. Above his signature he wrote the words "You and I will change the world to a peaceful world without shedding a drop of blood. The human species' problems are biological, and the solution will naturally have to be biological,"

Elon was so delighted and when he read the note he asked, "Charles, can I call you Dad?"

Charles was shocked by the question but said, "Call me whatever you want to. I'm sorry about the loss of your Dad. I know I cannot be as caring as your Dad, but I can always try my best," He replied, really feeling so close to this boy.

Well Charles felt such an immediate strong bond with Elon and they almost had a similar story to tell. After visiting Elon at his foster home and talking to the foster parents, he did all the necessary paperwork and adopted Elon.

He had some scars on his face, but nothing compared to Charles. He was a very sharp boy and Charles started working with him and taught him almost as much as he knew, mostly in his lab. We could say Elon taught Charles everything he knew. Right! They became extremely close and Elon was with Charles all the time and would not leave him alone.

Charles had to go on a trip to Chima and took Elon with him. They met Chen in a coffee shop. Let's listen in as Charles, Chen and Elon are eavesdropping on two passionate Chimese of different persuasion are talking about their own country, surprisingly in good English. Maybe speaking in English would prevent others around them to understand them since they feared their own government spying on them…a norm in Chima and all communist countries.

"You know our government has been very smart dealing with these stupid Americans…I mean American government. When I was taking a course in economics we learned about the concept of Adam Smith's Invisible Hand," The boy told the girl.

Charles, Chen and Elon became more curious and continued listening in.

"The concept is very simple…rather than having a central planning system for production and distribution of goods, like we do here, in those capitalist countries they rely on individualism. Freedom of production as well as consumption is the rule, and this gives each individual the courage to plan for himself and provide for his family. As a result the whole society benefits," The boy said, and they got up and walked away as they were discussing the concept in more detail.

"Charles you know this 'Invisible Hand' that they talked about has really been a blessing for Chima. It has been the main driving force for the rise of Chima to the point of almost taking over the United States," Chen said.

"Are you kidding me Chen? You have a central planning system here and no invisible hand is at work here. That concept only works in capitalist countries," Charles said.

"Exactly. You made my point Charles. We call it 'The Visible Hands of The Fools.' Isn't that sad? It means cheating by Chima, and the fools not only won't notice it, they love it. Stupidity has no limits. Sorry about that Charles. Your government has been simply stupid. The invisible hand works within your capitalist system and between capitalist countries. When you deal with adversaries like Chima, that becomes the most dangerous weapon against you.

Chima buys whatever they want from your big companies…their most secret of secrets. All those companies want is money, and Chima has a lot of it. Chima made advances by taking care of U.S. companies' shareholders but at the long-term expense of the U.S. government and American people," Chen explained.

So now Elon is learning economics and foreign policy. Let's continue listening as Chen explains more.

"Chima pays these companies whose intention is just the shareholder's interest and they will give Chima what Chima needs…intellectual properties and patent rights. Chima knows that they could even buy out the U.S. politicians. They have in the past and they will in the future. Come to think of it, the invisible hand becomes the most dangerous threat to the U.S. national security. Very simply, it is 'Company or Country.' Chima has been winning and the U.S. has been losing for over the past twenty five years or so," Chen says.

Chen wanted to conclude his remarks, but then Charles asked what he thought about U.S. versus Chima in military strength.

"You should not compare Chima and the United States of America's military in simple capability differentials or their military hardware, biolab, database maintenance, or computing capabilities. One could be so strong and have good intention. Another could be not as strong and stupid with malice intention. Chima knows that they have to win their war with the west in stages. First they have to weaken the fabric of the western society, using their imbedded agitators and thousands of agents and massive hacking. Stealing is Chima's specialty," Chen said, confiding in Charles. They finished their talk.

So, Chima gets their action into higher gear and started abusing Chen's friendship with Charles to their advantage and approached Chen to see if he can use their friendship to help Chima in coming up very quickly with some urgently needed vaccines. Even though Chima uses CRISPR technology among others, they still lacked some specific capabilities in rapid genetic engineering, Charles' lab did not.

The difficulty is that when it came to gene expression to produce specific protein, or spike, sometimes it is not just one single gene that expresses to make a single protein, but many or sometimes a society of genes contribution is needed to produce certain proteins or antibodies. Charles' knowledge in such an advanced field was unmatched in RNA and DNA based genetic sequencing and manipulating viral genes and proteins…a specialty that is needed for vaccine development. Chima's main weakness compared to Charles was the huge amount of data related to interactions between some twenty-two thousand human genes, but Charles' lab had that.

Charles gets more serious and studies Chima's communist party's manifesto and reads their national anthem and the speeches of their leaders and their obvious intent to take over the world...not hidden, but in plain sight. Finally, Chima tells Chen that he can offer fifty billion dollars...half paid in advance for the development of a few vaccines to Chima. The deal is confirmed, only under one condition...the absolute secrecy is not compromised.

Charles considers rejecting the funds but then again Chima has not given him any limitations and loss of control over his lab work. Strangely though Chima's agents secretly had given him an indication that maybe his blood has been found at a murder scene. Charles was shocked when he was told of that by an informer. But now he is scared that if they spread even the slightest rumor about this or arrest him for any baseless murder, that by the time he proves his innocence his lab work falls apart, and he won't even be able to protect his own country if Chima uses a bioweapon to attack the U.S.

All Chima wants is the result and Chen assures Chima that with the good relationship with Charles he will get the result. After all this is supposedly for the benefit of the world population and not against it, so why should he reject it?

Chen gives some data files and the five sets of viruses, the DNA and RNA data related to the viruses to Charles without realizing that a few DNA nucleotide bases were intentionally changed by Chima CDC. Chima's thinking was that if they get the Vaccines with the nucleotides deleted, they can modify them themselves to work with the viruses' DNAs when they add back the nucleotides.

But the fact that there were five viruses at a time raised Charles' suspicion as to the Chinese intent. Can it be malicious? He wondered why they would indicate that his blood may have been found in a murder scene. He knows he has not killed anyone. But how about Innocenti? After all their DNA is just about the same. He is doubting whether he should go to the FBI and tell them about this whole thing, but he does not see any urgency to that. After all he is producing vaccines, not viruses.

Chima transferred the twenty-five billion dollars down payment through the Chimese controlled banks and the transfer data was deleted overnight from the clearing houses by the transferee banks by a few Chimese agents, strategically placed within the U.S. Central Bank and the banking system. The US government did not even notice the money transfer. Stupid or what? For Chima, with so many agents, this type of thing is a piece of cake. They probably have them all over, even in our CDC.

Charles and his lab started the work and the secrecy was maintained. Only Charles and Chen knew where the viruses had come from. Charles and his lab very quickly realized that there were a few missing DNA nucleotides and corrected the sequences. After all, he has a vast number of bioassays and a huge database on gene interactions. It was a very laborious and time-consuming effort even with their fastest computer system.

The secrecy documents he had signed were related to all types of vaccines: live vaccines, inactivated vaccines, sub-unit, recombinant, polysaccharide, and conjugate vaccines, that use proteins or other pieces of the virus. The document also gave Chima protection rights for findings in his research pertaining to preclinical, clinical, manufacturing, and distributions. Chima's Liberation Army controls it all and they have covered all required bases. They had been planning this so precisely for an exceptionally long time and they think they have Charles in their grip.

Chapter 8
Freewill

Another Quantum Jump takes us to Elon and his friend discussion the subject of Freewill.

Late in the afternoon on this pleasant sunny day Elon was talking to his friend, Darnel, who was also a very smart boy. They were just about the same age. They were sitting on a bench in this beautiful park. Charles was sitting a few yards away from them and was listening to these two talented boys talking about the fascinating subject of Freewill.

"Elon, we know that subject of Freewill is so important for us. Everyone talks about it and so many books have been written on the subject by philosophers and scientists, apparently it is an important subject. Do you want to talk about it a bit?" Darnel asked.

"Of course. We kill people, put them in jail for life or fine them because of it. We have seen attorneys and Judges rule in courts on many cases as they discuss whether the person acted with intention or not. They bring out the insanity defense, claiming that the person was insane and did not know what he was doing, or his actions were not intentional...so it is an important subject," Elon said and continued.

"Ok Darnel, so let's discuss whether humans have and can exercise freewill or not. Just kicking some ideas around...and not a feisty debate...let's just discuss humans, not animals and plants," Elon suggested to Darnel.

"Ok great, if that is the case then we probably don't need to go any further, Elon. You just assumed that we already have what is so casually called 'freewill' by deciding to have this debate and for it not to be a feisty one. We made three choices, Number one, we made a decision to debate or not to debate. Secondly, we made a decision to make it friendly and not feisty. And third, we also excluded animals and plants. So that makes three intentional decisions on our part. We made a few choices out of the available alternatives. So isn't this exercising our so called freewill?" Darnel asked.

"I wish it were that easy, but unfortunately it is not. Anytime we talk, our state of mind changes and each word that we utter is selected among so many words. If freewill is a change in state of mind we are continuously exercising it. We made a choice to talk and not be silent. As we talk we are selecting words from our memory and putting them in the right sequence to make sense, so in a way we can say that without memory there were no alternatives available to us to choose from," Elon responded.

"Let's talk about it at a higher level. A simple naïve way of looking at it is for me to say that I decide to raise my hand. I did, so therefore I have freewill," Darnel mused.

Elon loved these conversations and added to it saying, "The basic question is whether we are so called *free* to decide between available alternatives and therefore can change the Universe's course and its physical shape. *Or* is it that the future is fixed, and like a machine it is taking its course just unwinding without us controlling it. If we can make a choice between alternatives, then can we make the choice *freely* from forces of the natural world?"

Darnel jumped in with vigor as he said, "Yes, we are physical, though biological beings. Anytime we chose an alternative we are shaping and changing the Universe,"

"Well, some philosophers believe that the world is deterministic because we cannot change the natural laws governing the Universe or their effect on us. I think they are wrong. They don't realize that we do not change any of the forces. We just *use* those laws. The good news is that we control those laws as well. The same laws that govern us…we govern them in many ways as well. We are a part of the Universe," Elon said.

"Exactly. We don't have to 'change' or 'control' the laws of nature to exercise our freewill. All we have to do is to 'use' those laws. We are a part of those laws…not separate from them anyway. We are not isolated from the Universe…we are intertwined with it. We are a part of its whole," Darnel said.

"One of the difficulties confronting us is our lack of complete knowledge about the natural laws…about our conscious mind and the definitions of 'free' and what we mean by 'will.' I think we need to change the title to "willed as we will' or 'freewilled as we freewill,' or 'controlling while being controlled.' If we go with these definitions then the question of freewill become more digestible," Elon said.

"What do you mean by "controlled while being controlled"? Darnel asked.

"Well, we know that this is a relational Universe, as all parts of it play together as a whole, each affecting each other in many fields. Granted, the effects may be smaller or larger, but they do affect the wholesomeness of it all. No part is isolated in any vacuum. Even its so called vacuum is full of energy. Let's assume that the whole Universe was a piece of a circular rope, and you are located in it too. It is full of energy…jiggling and shaking. Yes, you are in it and it shapes you…it jiggles you, but you also jiggle and vibrate the whole. They control you, but you control them as well. This is exactly what is happening here. We control them and they control us. Therefore the question, or the word 'freewill'…meaning free from forces, loses its meaning. It becomes an irrelevant word," Elon explained.

Darnel raised an eyebrow and paused a moment before adding, "So…let's limit our discussion based on knowledge of those forces, knowing that our knowledge about the world is not complete. Therefore we don't know what forces exert themselves on us. We know a little bit, but we do not fully understand the characteristics of those unknown forces…like the dark matter and dark energy. We only know about 5% of the Universe and the rest is still unknown. So therefore their interaction with us is unknown. And we still don't have a theory of everything, so not all known forces and fields are reconciled with gravity,"

"But those forces are stronger than us therefore can we say we exercise less control on them than they on exert on us?" Elon asked.

"Again it depends on how we use them, let us say that you are sitting in the middle of a very rocky but shaky mountain, if you use a few calories and move a middle size stone, you can make an avalanche of many stones coming down, so you used your energy but use the potential energy of so many stones and your tiny action caused a major action on the mountain," Darnel replied.

"Well, since the question involves our biology…especially a brain or the so called mind, then the question becomes a science-based biological question.

We know that there are no exact sciences, so I don't think we can come up with a definite answer with one hundred percent accuracy. Everything we know about the world is our best estimation, right?" Elon asked.

"Well, having the ability to choose and exercising it are two different and separate things are they not?" Darnel asked.

"I don't think so. They are both events…they are mental states. To decide is a nanosecond of a second decision, but to make it continual becomes an exercise. It is a continuation…just like when you utter a sentence, selecting one word after another. When you make a decision so many things happens in your brain. We know the decision is your brain's decision, but we don't know at what level of consciousness and with exactly what neuron or neuronal network it started, using fMRI we can see the area that activates but we don't exactly know, that is all," Elon replied.

"So we agree that they are both mental states, whether they are continual or not?" Darnel asked.

"Yes Darnel, and as I said before, without having memory you could not even know about the alternatives. So if memory plays such an important role and if a person is in his late state of Alzheimer's, then does he not have any freewill of his own? Furthermore at what stage of developing Alzheimer does the person lose his control, it becomes a legal question, so even the law becomes a part of the freewill discussion. You know, one of the problems we face in any experiment or discussion is that it is difficult to isolate a specific experience from many other factors. So many alternatives play into this freewill discussion. Let's not forget that we can only choose between the alternatives. Most of the time, the availability of those alternatives is not under our control. You cannot decide to move your third hand if you only have two," Elon mused as he held up his hands and pretending trying summon a third.

Darnel laughed and mimicked the movement along with him. When their laughter faded Darnel added more thoughts. "Yes, even if you go with that example, you have to have a hand to start with. You have to have a brain to make that decision and you have to have energy to raise your hands. Trillions of things have to exist. Even you, yourself have to exist and your being here was not your decision,"

Elon patted his friend on the shoulder with a smile. "Of course, I know that. The old physics that were based on a deterministic world are no more.

The Quantum Physic is now our latest knowledge and understanding of the world and natural forces. Depending on how you tally them, let's go with seventeen quantum fields...*plus* gravity...until that knowledge base is changed. So for now, we know that in our Quantum world there is always a measure of indeterminacy built into the fabric of the Universe and the probabilities rule. Unless we want to make a philosophical sacrifice and claim that an unnatural power transcends the laws of nature, therefore giving us the power to choose. But we have not seen any delegation by a moral agent or God, and so if we assume that, it will be a big sacrifice and a huge departure from science,"

"Well, if we believe in a *mind* outside of our physical brain, then it will be a free-floating mind and that is hard to believe in. So far as we know, our consciousness is a physical interaction of our collective neurons. You can call it emergence, but we cannot call it a free-floating mind," Darnel exclaimed and continued. Now, if the world is probabilistic, how can we say we can control it? And if it is deterministic, then we definitely have no control over it, right? Elon, do you agree with me that those probabilities are just probabilities and cannot be predictable with one hundred percent accuracy?"

Elon shrugged his shoulders and replied. "Well...nothing is one hundred percent predictable. The name "probability" says it all...but if we can change the probabilities then we can say that we do have some measure of freewill. But you know, some philosophers believe that freewill and determinism are mutually compatible,"

Darnel squinted at Elon for a moment before pressing on. "Ok, give me an example."

"Well, if you don't buy a lotto ticket you will not win anything, right? But if you buy all the lotto tickets, will you definitely win?" Elon asked.

"Not necessarily, Elon. Assume that we buy all of the tickets and then there comes a huge Earthquake, and everyone dies. Even though this chance is minimal...but it can theoretically happen...you may lose the winning ticket and cannot prove that you were the winner," Darnel said.

"That may be so Darnel, but your decision to buy a few tickets may have been controlled by biases that controlled your decision...the biases that had been built into your psyche. For example, you wanted to become rich because of the jealousy you had by seeing all your friends rich, but you are not rich yourself," Elon said.

Darnel stopped him with and held his hand up, waving him away. "But we are not talking about the reasons behind your action. After all these biases went into your consideration, you still decided to do that didn't you"?

"That is true, but your unconscious mind has a lot to say when you "decide" on something. For example, in the morning…out of habit, you wear your clothes and do not go to your office nude. Bias and habits all framed into a neuronal circuit act on this without you even thinking. So where is the control in this case? The will that was controlled by biases is built into your memory," Elon explained.

"But after taking all of these biases and everything else into account at the end of the day it was still *you* who made the decision to buy tickets and wear whichever clothes you picked out. They were all freewill action on your part, right?" Darnel asked in return.

"Not necessarily," Elon replied. "You know that there are studies made by major reputable institutions, like The Planck Institute, and confirmed by others…that when we think that we have made a conscious choice, our physical brain had already made that decision a fraction of a second before we *thought* we made that decision. So is this an illusion on our part that we are the one deciding? The feeling of deciding may not be a true choice of selecting between alternatives. Like the feeling of winning one million dollars without actually having won it…our brain could easily be tricked, you know. Our eyes especially can be tricked…and that is one of our major senses that the brain uses to 'decide'. So the whole thing becomes fuzzier probabilistically,"

The discussion was getting intense, but both boys remained engaged with a friendly and thoughtful tone. Darnel commented as he looked into the park. "I know…our freewill is based on our interactions of our senses with the world. It takes time to make decisions and exercise them…and that brings uncertainty or delay into making free choices. Even our sense of touch comes into play, as it takes longer for you to sense the touch if I touch your nose versus your toe. So, let's do an exercise. If I told you to close your eyes and raise your hand when I touch you…and you don't know where I will be touching you…on your nose or your toe…so when you feel the first touch, you are to raise your hand and when you feel the second touch, you bring your hand down. Okay, so if the first touch is on your leg and the second touch on your nose, I could calculate exactly the time difference between the two as to when they each reach your brain and you probably won't even raise your hand. The control becomes your state of mind that is biologically based on other factors. It can confuse your will as my actions control and cancel even your senses. You could not use your senses to make that decision, and if your leg was longer this whole thing would be different.

"You are right…who knows, maybe so many forces are continually cancelling our other senses without us even noticing it," Elon confirmed and continued. "The whole thing depends on our definition of the word 'control' In other words, can we call it 'control' while we are being controlled? If that is the case, then we can accept that we have control. Furthermore, we have to answer a basic question. By having freewill, do we mean the exercise or intent to do something, like a change in our mental state or the outcome of a decision?" Elon asked, with just as much intensity as his friend.

"Maybe under the exact identical circumstances, we make a choice between alternatives, but there are never ever identical circumstances in a purely scientific base. Your physics are a part of what makes those alternatives and you can never really take yourself out of those alternatives, so therefore you are affecting it. Your physical body affects making those alternatives available or not. Again, you control…while being controlled," Darnel reasoned.

"Let's say you are driving a car and you exercise control by deciding to turn the wheel, right? Does the word 'control' mean that your mental state changed, and you made a decision as a result? Are we talking about your mental decision to turn the wheel or your intent to make a turn to go to your friend's house?" Elon asked.

"Both are mental decisions. The decision to go to your friend's house came first. The intent is more important than the outcome here when it comes to answering the question of whether we have Freewill or not," Darnel explained.

"If so, would you still say that you have absolute control over your decision turning the wheel," Elon asked, with a gleam in his eye.

"Well there are trillions and trillions of outside influences in us that control us as well. But the good news is that we also control them. Who made the road? We did, as a society," Darnel replied.

"So, you are saying that control is also spread between people…communities…and nations, right?" Elon asked.

"Yes of course," Darnel stated.

"So, you agree that many biases that are imbedded in our psyche exert control over us don't you?" Elon asked, more slowly this time.

"What biases are you talking about?" Darnel asked Elon.

"Biases created by family…the city or country…and as a species. They have formed so many networks in our brain controlling our actions. We don't go nude to our daily job, do we? We are free to do that, but that word free is so controlled by our family and societal biases that it loses its meaning. The biases control us. It's not us controlling them. It is like priming…being controlled subconsciously," Elon said.

"But I still have control and can decide to go nude," Darnel said, with a sly smile.

Elon gave his friend a laugh to humor him. "You do…but apparently the other forces overcome our decision and therefore our control, so would you still call it control"?

"When we use the word free, we should answer the question of what we are referring to as free. Free from what? All-natural forces and biases? You know that we can never ever do that," Darnel explained.

"But Darnel, those natural forces and biases cannot free themselves from us either, don't you agree?" Elon asked.

"I agree one hundred percent…unless…if we believe in supernatural forces giving us control over our actions…like a god or another power outside of the realm of physical laws, then we can say we have Freewill. I need to be careful not to use 'one hundred percent', we know that we can't say that." Darnel said.

"But then we would be talking nonsensical concept things that are not even pseudoscience. Like another god controlling the first god…all nonsense," Elon said.

"How about randomness and chaos. How do they play into the discussion of freewill?" Darnel asked.

"Well…we have limitations understanding them too. We do not know if randomness or chaos exists in the interactions of the forces…or better to say quantum fields, in the universe and their interactions with gravity. Simply because the result is incalculable, we cannot label them as purely random or chaotic. And we have the Quantum indeterminacy and uncertainty, which leaves a secret that we may never ever get to know…a secret about the nature of reality. This is the problem with observation," Elon replied.

"Let's take a coin…and if I ask you what chances are as to how the coin will fall on the floor you will probably say one of three things. Heads, tails, or on its circled edge. But there are trillions of ways it will come down. See, the question was how it will come down…not what side. So these things are all a matter of how the question is posed, and it is the same for freewill. To me, it is an incomplete question," Darnel said, as he leaned back and put his hands behind his head.

Elon looked at him out of the corner of his eyes. "Can we say freewill evolves? I mean…as a newborn we were not aware of our actions. Our Freewill evolved…atom by atom, neuron by neuron, ionic pulse by ionic pulse. There is a sequence of evolution taking charge of our actions. Not necessarily in this sequence, first, we became aware of space. Then we became aware of others, and next we became aware of ourselves. Then we evolved more and became aware of our awareness. But becoming aware of our awareness does not mean at that instant of time we took total control of our destiny or our actions. Our fate is not controlled by our genes, but by genes affected by epigenetic forces. So outside forces have something to say about our decisions that are genetic related. Even our DNA evolved by these epigenetic forces. Genes do not determine our destiny. They only have some influence," Elon said. He sat back and looked at Darnel with a smile as he also laced his fingers behind his head and began to close his eyes. Darnel elbowed him a little with a chuckle and Elon chuckled back.

"Hey guys…we need to go. We have to be at the restaurant by six and we're almost late. Good discussion, boys. Let's exercise our freewill and go. Did you guys find out whether we do have freewill or not?" Charles asked, with curiosity.

"Well we would have wished to continue our discussion but your freewill overwrote ours. And we need to be there on time since it is bad to be late when our guests are waiting for us. To be punctual is a bias that we do not wish to overcome or overrule. So let that bias take charge and let's go. It is good to be on time," Elon told everyone.

Chapter 9

Final Attack

Enough of freewill discussion, let's go back to our main story with Chima.

Suddenly, the radio communication system for all States in The United States fails and shuts down for five seconds. What does that mean? Five seconds for you and I may not mean much, but for the country it has a huge implication. The head of the military tells the president that two key U.S. communications satellites have been hit and are downed. The US blames Chima, but Chima denies any involvement with this. Rubbas also denies any involvement. Well the United States has been smart and had a backup plan and the backup satellites had immediately taken over the downed satellites. The FBI, the CIA, and the military started analyzing the five second failure and come up with a plan to prevent it from happening again. But can they? They also got the FCC involved. Federal Communications Commission is in charge of regulating interstate and international communications by wire, radio, television cable and most importantly, satellites.

The President was told that this was most probably caused by Chima and not the country of Rubbas. He gets on the phone with Chima's President and basically warns him that the U.S. has the capability to down their satellites as well, to cause the same problem for Chima and to shut down their communication system. This was just to put them on notice, as if they already did not know that. The U.S. files a complaint with the United Nations Security Council. Do we expect anything resolved at the Security Council where our competitors have veto power?

Let's Quantum Jump to the FBI office as TC urgently goes to the Director, Nikola again. What will he feed the FBI this time around? TC leaves a note, a letter, and a tape recording, and then leaves very quickly. The note simply shows the code word TVOOPFTSTVOTW.

The FBI have their computer gurus trying to see if these combinations will result in a meaningful sentence. Among many, the computer comes up with two long sentences. The first one said, "To Value Our Own People First To Sustain The Value Of Their Wages." The second sentence was, "To Vaccinate Our Own People First Then Spread The Virus on The West." Amazing! Shocking! Scary!

But what do the sentences really mean and what did the letter say? The letter that TC left with the FBI had the following few paragraphs written in plain English.

This is the letter in a few paragraphs:

A. If Chima must exploit or ignore international rules they will. Who can or will stop them?

B. Chima's leaders know that their own military is extremely strong but if they ever start a nuclear war with the west it will be mutually devastating. The communist party's strategists know that Bio War is the cheapest and the most effective weapon.

C. They also know that the most dangerous risk is a pandemic that it can overwhelm their own medical system and cause a serious downfall of Chima's different regions, killing their own countrymen. The communist party been planning for a long time to overwhelm the West. To achieve it, Chima had assembled thousands of top strategists together and let them work on a master plan. Their problem has been that they were still lacking the genetic engineering capability to develop the right vaccine for five viruses at the same time. In a Bio war the enemy has to be overwhelmed. Even though Chima could not make vaccines, they had been able to manipulate certain viruses to make them deadlier, and to target five various body organs.

D. As part of their plan Chima had been at work to abuse race relations in the U.S. in order to weaken the fabric of the U.S. society. When the Chimese master plan is implemented, these unsettled racial and social tensions will be helpful for an easier implementation of their master plan. The intention is to exert as much structural and societal damage first.

E. They must weaken the enemy's military first. Their war simulations show they can win a war in the South Chima Sea because they know attacking U.S. interest in Chima's backyard is non defendable by the U.S. forces. They know the U.S. will not risk their larger interest, which is to protect their own residents and other major assets around the world.

F. Chima knows that the European countries are not mentally capable of being engaged in a major war with Chima. They have been spoiled having another master, through NATO, protecting them for years. Chima is not worried about NATO. They trust the backing of their friend, the country of Rubbas in case they need help to deal with NATO. Chima knows Rubbas is feeding Europe with natural gas and oil, so they can easily be manipulated and persuaded not to enter the war. All Rubbas needs to do is to turn the gas knob to the "OFF" position!

G. Chima knows that if you want to go to a bio-type conflicts and use bioweapons, their own population of 1.3 billion people can die too. Their master plan had included having some one hundred fifty thousand agents installed in strategic places in the U.S. and Europe, who were constantly giving them feedback. Their discussion and plan talked about five viruses that have been fully developed in their labs after major studies had been done for their function, speed of spread, and the bodily organs they will attack.

H. The related human genes are Gene actg1 that affects skeletal muscles structure and function, Gene SFTCP that affects pulmonary function, Gene HFE, regulating iron absorption and energy, Gene SOD1, affecting neurons, and gene Gimap5, that affects the immune system. They are also working on another virus that affects the vision, GRIA4. Even though viruses are named by the International Committee on Taxonomy of Viruses, Chima chose a different naming method and has named the five viruses based on their nucleic acid sequence.

I. Those are the genes. The related viruses were named by Chima as VR1ACTG1, VR2SFTCP, VR5HFE, VR3SOD1, and VR7GImap5. The abbreviations are VR for the Virus, the number after VR for their generation, and lastly the name of the gene.

This is a major and serious warning to the west. I cannot go into any more detail. Beware of the seriousness of "The Power Of Agency." The attack can come any day, any week, but soon.}

That was the end of the letter.

So, this letter summarized the intent of Chima attacking the West using bioweapons. It is scary, but is it true? Have they been planning for this for some time without the west knowing? Had they used or abused Charles, and if so... how, how long, and why? And when will the attack come? Why is the U.S. not prepared?

Once again TC goes to the FBI office and gives them some additional information. How about the recording that TC left at the FBI? And what did that show? The FBI cannot see it yet since it had a code to open. TC will bring it to the FBI later. We can't see the video right now, but we can talk or Quantum Jump and see the video later, we hope.

TC also gives them a recording of a few Chinese officials in extremely high positions, talking amongst each other. The recording was played by Nikolas' staff and translated. It said the following, and clearly shows the intent of the communist country. Let's read the summary together.

"Heck, we don't give a damn if our feeder companies working in the West are charged with intellectual property theft or cyber security and human rights violations…as long as even 10 percent of our surveillance work is successful we will call it a full success. They say that our source and feeder companies' wireless network is a back door for the Chimese government…well they are right on target. We care for results,"

"They are afraid of our feeder companies and the 5G capability. As one of their leaders once said, 'they ain't seen nothing yet'. We ask them what is five times two and they can't even calculate that because they have such stupid leaders. They don't know what is 10 hooked with an alphabet."

After the FBI reads the note and the letter, Nikola very quickly assembled a staff with the military leaders to analyze the information. They are now getting more nervous. Now five viruses and five times two with an alphabet code gives an indication of a 10G network, but the west is hardly capable of establishing a 5G network. Has Chima developed a 10G? Is the 10G network established just for their military use? Impossible. Is it misinformation?

Since a few other chatters indicated that a U.S. naval carrier may be targeted by Chima, and if hit it will definitely be drowned, the military gets scared. After consulting with the President, they reposition three of the biggest U.S. carriers and submarines to the South Chima Sea. Now the United States of America wants to show the world its magnificent naval and air power. Chima's best guess is that the U.S. government will not start a nuclear war if their big ship is gone. Chima knows that this is their backyard and they can easily fend off any non-nuclear attack on their territory.

Since 2006, the Chima's Liberation Army Navy, with the cooperation and agreement with their counterparts, had been getting Chima ready by increasing the number of submarines and their capabilities. Will they use one of their nuclear submarines in the South Chima Sea? What if the counterattack engages Chima and drowns their nuclear-powered submarines? But they are sure the U.S. will not escalate fully, and they are willing to take that risk. At the most they will lose one of their bigger ships, but not a nuclear-powered one. The U.S. knows not to touch any of those.

All at the same time many explosions happen within the military bases in the United States and their NATO Allies. The US and their Allies are puzzled. Is this the "Power of Agency" that TC had indicated before? Did it mean the use of agents within the enemy's system to weaken the strength of their adversary? One step at a time before the master plan goes into effect.

On the nightly news networks, the anchors report that Chima has hit and drowned one of the two biggest U.S. naval carriers, carrying sixty airplanes. The big ship and all fighter planes are sunk. All but fifty crew members have been drowned and are still listed as missing in action. The Naval Nimitz-class aircraft carrier is gone. People think that it could be another "fake news" story. The U.S. military immediately engages the Chinese on a counterattack and hits two smaller Chinese ships that carried a total of seventy fighter jets, and all were drowned. Some of the US fighter airplanes and those of Chima scramble and start a dogfight in the air on a counterattack. The U.S. downs ten Chimese fighter jets and Chima downs two of the U.S. airplanes. All pilots are declared dead. Chima downs one of United States' planes, the important EP-3 reconnaissance plane. We know one thing…one fact…our biggest ship is gone, and the situation is extremely dangerous.

The two leaders get on the emergency phone and agree to stop the aggression. Will there be a Chinese bio attack coming next? All Chinese, and United States nuclear submarines and military bases in the U.S. and NATO countries are on their highest alert. Every second matters and any mistake or miscalculation could be deadly for the world.

The President goes on TV right away to report the attack and the counterattack. People realize that the reported news was correct, and panic starts within the country. The highest degree of food shortage and supplies follows. Shelves are empty and there is little food in supermarkets and very little water. The country has not seen anything like this and isn't prepared for this. The National Security Advisor, U.S. Military, State Department leaders, and all State governors quickly assemble to see what needs to be done next.

Both leaders use the attacks as propaganda on their own people. The U.S. military leaders are devastated but cannot fully accept and show their defeat. U.S. military knows what this means. On the surface we defeated them as far as the numbers of downed airplane and ships, but they know that this means

Chima:1, United States of America: 0…at least so-far. Two small ships versus the biggest? The downing of more jets by the U.S. is not that significant on a military scale. Chima is happy. Two military and State Department groups from each country start talking peace.

But is this the start of their big plan? A plan that had been cooking by over 1,500 Chinese strategists? What will come next? A Chinese version of "Shock and Awe," but a Shock and Bio-Awe?

We care about the killing of Anna, but in wars many get killed and not that many people care. What a nice kind red planet we live on! No other choice…killing and waste is unfortunately imbedded in our universal bio processes. Maybe Richard Dawkins and Innocenti were right saying so many bad things about a creator. Or maybe it is designed by nature as unfortunately suffering is a part of nature. We can't just go to another planet and start a peaceful world, but that is one of Charles' desires as he had written in his book, Changing all Red Planets to Blue! Is Elon going to help him with that?

Back to reality. Now the FBI and the military start believing TC and other defectors who had told them about the intent of Chima planning to drown a big U.S. ship. Their confidence in TC goes much higher. He has been correct, and his information is now corroborated by action on the Chinese part. How serious should the U.S. President and military advisors take this? Can any bio attack be corroborated by any U.S. spies in Chima? For the United States, it has been exceedingly difficult to penetrate the secrecy that the communists of Chima had developed throughout their government.

We are getting closer to the end of our story, but we still don't know who killed Anna. Why are we talking about Chima? Why is Charles being involved with Chima? Has he been selling his country? Where is Innocenti?…still in jail? Where are Buzz and his parents?

Chapter 10

Prayers

Let's see what Buzz has been doing lately. Our Quantum Jump takes us to a church where he is debating about the effect of Prayers on people. A Priest named Christopher, who was the priest of a local church had invited another preacher, Gene Zaman, to speak with him. Gene Zaman is a man of God who left the church because his belief in God had changed. The three of them start going at it. It will be an interesting debate between a man of God, a scientist astronaut and a converted nonbeliever. So, let's listen in as they start their debate about the effect of Prayers in front of some 500 church members. Christopher introduced everyone to the audience and let Buzz start the discussion.

"Well, brother Christopher, if you don't mind we will call you Chris… you know that true and deep knowledge always comes handy and our deeper knowledge and understanding of the effect of Prayers is no different. I have to be honest with you…I love science and the precision that goes with it. So can we expect we'll be able to find out the positive and negative effect of Prayers on people?" Buzz asked.

Now Chris responds. "Of course, we should all expect that, but as a scientist you are probably trying to take away our right to pray but why?" Chris told Buzz and the audience.

"Oh no, not at all. If you enjoy praying and if you think it has a good effect on you then there is no reason you should stop praying. There is more to know about the effect of prayers than we think. Normally we pray when we need something that we cannot easily reach by our own means or when we are seeking a higher justice or desire of improvements in our lives. We believe more in god when we need something, but when the need goes away we sometimes forget about him or her or it," Buzz said.

"You are right brother Buzz. Prayers always seek intervention by a supernatural power to improve a situation for health, food, financial improvement, or the stress that a divorced parent suffers when the other parent so selfishly takes away the child and moves to another state, so sickening, insane. But we know that prayers work, so what is wrong with that?" Chris asked.

"We pray to god when major devastations like Earthquakes, hurricanes, or epidemics hit nations. The very same devastations that your own God imposed on us…the so called 'act of God'…why would your loving God act like that to start with? Is he trying to force us to beg him for his own mass killings?" Buzz asked.

"But if it helps the victims mentally then why not?" Chris said.

"Brother Chris, it does not work. If prayers worked, we could save so much in electricity usage and save a lot of money. Furthermore, if getting mental satisfaction is the main reason for it, the murderers, the rapists and people who lie also get mental satisfaction," Buzz states.

"Did you say we would save on electricity? Wow……wow brother Chris! What in the world are you talking about brother?" Chris asked, in somewhat of a mocking tone.

"Well, we think the prayers work but in ways that we cannot measure their effectiveness. We start abusing it, like praying for peace or praying for rain. I will only believe in effectiveness of prayers if I put a kettle or a pot on the stove and pray for it to heat up and I see it boiling. Do you think it will? I bet you that if I pray for a million years it will not come to a boiling point, it will not even warm up, if it did, everyone would use the 'prayer method' and not turn the gas range on," Buzz said.

"But Buzz, we are not talking about a kettle, we are talking about putting our warm hands on other people's arms, holding hands in their time of needs… That, combined with prayers gives them an assurance that we are there for them, and that we are sharing their pain. As a scientist you should know better. It has a biological effect on their mind, does it not?" Chris asked.

"Of course. Sharing their pain is good, but why bring Jesus and God into it? Just let people know that you are supporting them…like opening your check book or in a very warm caring way. Even putting your warm hand on them…not just one hand, but both," Buzz said and continued. "Let's talk about some examples and see how prayers can result in the death of others. My dear brother, not all prayers are positive and not all prayers reach the intended purpose. Without having bad intentions, our prayers…if they work… negatively affect others…directly or indirectly…and some are just purely selfish. Almost all prayers fall in these groups and have an embedded meanness in them," Buzz said.

Gene, who had left the church and had seen so many things from the inside jumps into the conversation.

"The prayers performed by preachers and televangelists…who are good psychologists…are so much repeated that they have lost their true deep meanings. Have no doubt, brother that at the end of the prayers they normally ask for money. I was an insider in our churches, so I kind of know the tricks. They deepen their voice, use fluffy words, jump up and down, and talk in the so called tongue," Gene said.

"Well it works for the good of the church and society. Let me give you an example. Last year we had a bad water leak in the basement of the church, so I asked everyone to pray and ask our merciful Lord to help the church with the leak," Christopher said.

"So, did it work? Did your merciful Lord fix the leak?" Buzz asked.

"Of course. As a result of our prayers we started collecting money in that same Sunday service and we hired a plumber and we got it fixed," Chris replied.

"Well, a little reasoning about the leak with the members would have worked the same way. There would not have been a need if you asked God to become your plumbing company sending his plumber. Why do we need to ask an unknown god to help and why resort to fear?" Buzz asked.

"I did not resort to fear. I only resorted to hope, for a better tomorrow, and it worked," Chris said.

"Of course preplanning and having insurance would have worked as well. Brother Chris, I remember a few years ago we had a major local drought and the main river going through our town almost dried out. The dam levels went drastically down. The governor of the State called on the residents to gather in front of the State Capitol to come and pray for rain. It is always an easy way out to pray…to compensate for your own lack of planning. Had he done a better job in water conservation…building more dams, the State would have been ready for lack of rain," Buzz said.

Gene again inserted himself into the conversation with some inside information.

"Brother Chris, I have seen many preachers at times asking the members to give the church some 'seed money' as they call it. Is that because they want to manipulate the crowd knowing that the word 'seed' has an embedded meaning in their mind for 'reaping' more from the same seed, therefore hope for more money for the church? Isn't this metal manipulation?" Gene asked and continued. "Of course, preachers…not you brother…are good psychologists and advertisers. The Viagra advertisers use more exposed women in their advertisements as men's weakness. The evangelists use people's weaknesses… their guilt," Gene said.

"Exactly. It's called 'priming.' Or you can call it manipulating people's freewill. You go to a movie theater and they artificially release a popcorn scent in the air. People, without realizing that they have been manipulated, go and buy popcorn," Buzz said, trying to back Gene with his comment.

"Of course, I have to promote my church. What do you want me to do… promote Islam in my church?" Chris replies.

"You just made my point brother. Have you ever heard the words 'Allahu Akbar' in any church? Have you ever heard a word praising Moses or Jesus in any Mosque? It has nothing to do with a self-declared god. It is all about controlling your own sect for your intended chosen biased purpose," Buzz said.

"Brother Buzz, you want to take away something good from a person's mind…something that gives them satisfaction…a deep pleasure. What do you plan or want to replace it with?" Chris asked Buzz and continued. "Just listen to these prayers that come from the heart of our church members. You will love their sincerity. They so enjoy it as sincere tears fall on their cheeks. To me it would be a sin to take away those pleasures and erase it from their mind. They yearn for peace and justice, they sincerely ask for food, for less killing. What is wrong with them saying, 'Heavenly God, I praise your Holy name, give me strength dear Lord, enough power to stand against the evil, keep me safe Lord from the works of the Satan trying to seep into my mind.' Or when they say 'Lord, grant us peace and justice, don't let the father or the mother take their children away when they go through divorce," Chris said.

"Exactly brother Chris, but don't forget that many who simply say 'Allahu Akbar' are also extremely sincere even when they savagely decapitate and cut off other people's heads. Are they also not your god's creatures? Are they not as sincere? They are enjoying it in their brain, even when they are acting like fools and murderers. Taking revenge is also a mental satisfaction that you so proudly supported a minute ago. This is either the evolution and natural selection at work or has it been designed by a mean-spirited creator?" Buzz continued.

"We pray for peace, but there are wars all over the world…so is your god not accepting these prayers? If your god was listening why do we have so many unfilled prayers? We all want peace, but at the same time we promote wars by believing in nationalism, flags, borders, lack of sacrifice between countries… giving uncontrolled powers to our elected officials," Gene said. "Brother Chris, prayers are a convenient way to satisfy our mind as they reinforce our belief that we have done our job showing our intent, albeit the convenient way. It is the easiest way out…escaping from taking responsibility or applying logic or reason. And then…when our prayers are not answered we go into more grief. Maybe God does not love me anymore or she just does not give a darn," Gene said.

"Are you two done with complaining about prayers, my brothers?" Chris asked.

"Well, not quite brother Chris. When we dig a bit deeper into the effect of prayers you see many hidden and mean messages with bad intent in them… unknown…or at least unrealized by the person saying the prayers," Buzz said.

"What negative effect brother Buzz?" A church member asked. Apparently, she had enough of listening to Buzz and Gene and she wanted to get involved in the discussion. She wanted them to stop insulting her loving God.

"Thank you for asking ma'am and let me give you an example. I'm sure you are a caring American. So let's imagine the son of an American couple is in a boxing match with a strong, young, Mexican boxer. The American family is sitting in a corner watching and praying for their son to win. To win means hitting hard. They scream their heart out for their son… 'hit, hit, upper, lower anywhere, hit, hit more, your opponent is falling, hit my dear son, he is bleeding and you are winning son…ten more seconds left…hit harder, come on, eight more seconds, one second'…and the buzzer goes off," Buzz said.

"So, what is wrong with wanting their son to win? It' a sport…a competition, is it not? Competition and sports are healthy and good," The lady explained.

"Yes ma'am, but I am not talking about the competition. I'm talking about the effect of prayers by the parents. They screamed and prayed, their son won, but the other guy has fallen bleeding all over, pronounced dead. Imagine at the time they were praying for their son to win they were also praying that the opponent goes down in blood or dies and ascends to your God's heaven. That is exactly what happened. God listened to the American family's prayers and the Mexican boy is dead. For some reason, the Mexican family's prayers did not reach or were ignored by God. So this poor Mexican family had sold their only car and spent thousands of dollars coming from south of Mexico to see their son win. Now they have a dead son to take back with them. Did the American family really mean to cause so much suffering for these poor people? Probably not, but that is exactly what they did. Do you see my point ma'am?" Buzz said and continued with some other negative effects of prayers.

"People pray for more food for their kids and family to show up on their dining table. Well, when they ask for more food they are actually and indirectly asking less food to go on other people's tables. More food for you taken out of the limited supply of food means higher demand for food resulting in higher prices for others," Buzz continued. "You pray for God to bring a surgeon to attend to your need, but the surgeon will be taken away from others…or at least demand for more surgery will result in a higher salary for the surgeon and less available time for others. Who pays for that? Others will," Buzz says.

Gene backed up Buzz and said, "All you good people…anytime you want to win… your hidden desire is for someone else to lose, creating a negative mood or effect on others. This escalates the negativity in relationship… whether you did it knowingly or unknowingly does not matter. And when this is at a national level for a country to win over other countries, it causes wars and naturally many dead people as we have seen in major wars," Gene said.

Chris thought of a good example to finally corner and check mate Buzz and Gene. "Brother Buzz, what if the sacrifice is of yourself? For example, this lady loves her husband so much and prays to her loving God to take away five years of her life and for each of those five years to add a day to her husband's life. How is that affecting others in a negative way? This wife and mother is so lovingly sacrificing her own life. Nobody else's food or health or bank account is in jeopardy," Chris said.

It looks like Buzz is finally cornered with this impossible question, let's see how he responds.

"Well this looks like a difficult situation. Ok, let's think about that a bit, gimme a second. Did she ever ask her children first? Imagine that the wife is a much more caring person than the husband and imagine their children don't like the father and they love their mother more. They couldn't possibly live without her. Let's say one of their children was born without arms and the daughter's day-to-day living depends on the mother and let's say the father didn't even care. Wouldn't the prayers adversely affect the daughter's life? God listened and shortened the mother's life and for every five years gave a few days to the father. Now the mother is gone, and you can guess the rest of the story," Buzz says and takes a deep breath, relieved.

Another church member is a bit outraged; she stands up and asks Buzz a question. "Mr. Armstrong do you not believe that there is a God, a creator sir?"

"No ma'am, I do not, why should I? If I force myself to believe in your God then I have to accept that the Earth and us were created some 4,000 years ago. Furthermore if I am a good person with all qualities a man should have what difference does it make whether I do or do not, especially if the purpose of your belief in God is to lead you to have moral standards,"

"But don't you think anything has to have a creator?" She asks.

"No, if you believe so then who created your God, another God?" Buzz asks in return.

"God has always been there, he is the divine, has created the Universe and time, has always been there without a creator," She said with confidence thinking that her God is supporting him in the argument, and who knows maybe he will.

"Well, if you think something can exist without a creator, then maybe this Universe existed without a creator, has always been an continue to be here," Buzz replied.

"Well why can't I use your own argument against you sir, if you think anything, the Universe, can exist without a creator, then maybe God had existed without a creator," Buzz feels he is being cornered. Can he come up with a persuasive counter argument?

"I agree with you that anything, you call it God, we call it Universe can exist without a creator,"

"So you agree that a God may exist Right?" She asked being so happy that she thinks she won the argument.

"Yes, but I think a couple of thousand gods exists, they always have, and they always will, and none of them are just or kind god," He replied.

"I think saying that is a sin, heresy and blasphemy are unforgivable sins and I don't want to argue with you anymore, I think you have a God problem sir," She said that and stiffly walked out of the church as everyone is watching.

"My dear friends, Buzz and Gene…let's go ahead and assume there are many Gods. I won't get upset like our dear lady who just left us. As long as you believe in the concept of God as your teacher…and who in the world said you always have to have the *best* teacher. To teach you math, for instance…any math teacher that you select will be as good under the circumstances. So any of those Gods as your moral teacher will be better than not having a God to lead you, right?" Christopher asked.

"Well not so quickly. A not-so-good teacher can teach you something that is not correct, so be careful as to which God you select to lead and teach you," Buzz replied.

They go through more discussion and then Christopher closes their meeting after thanking everyone and asks everyone to close their eyes and pray for their country, the USA, and for everyone's family, brother Chris and the church. People who believe in a just God never give up on prayers!

Now let's go back to our story…enough of complaining about god and prayers.

Chapter 11
The Downfall

Back to Chima's situation and their planned attack on the United States. How far back has Chima been planning for a bio attack? Is the U.S. ready? Does the U.S. have enough masks that work on five unknown viruses? Do the hospitals have enough bed and equipment? How long will it take to develop an effective vaccine?

The FBI knows that Charles has been going back and forth to Chima and they suspect that there is something going on between his lab, which is in many ways more sophisticated than our own CDC and Chima's CDC. His lab's capabilities are unmatched. So, they went ahead and got a FISA court order and start listening to Charles.

After listening to Charles and Chen the FBI realizes that he has been paid an exorbitant amount for developing some vaccines. Well, there is nothing wrong with that...after all, Chima has been paying other major companies for so many other technological property rights. Call it stealing or paying for products...it is that "Invisible Hand" acting in full force. You can call it "The 25 Year Bear Sleep of Our Smart Presidents" or another label. But had he violated the laws on money transfer?

Charles knew about the FISA Court. Could the court be manipulated to allow the FBI to listen in on this innocent Charles? Is Charles innocent? Has he been in cahoots with Chima against his own country and is Charles the murderer? Did he insert a device and neuronal networks in Innocenti's brain, causing Innocenti to kill Anna Rodriguez? Your guess is as good as anyone's.

Back to TC, the informer, as he is now an exceptionally reliable source. He tells the FBI to be wary and careful of a code DV. But what is meant by this code DV? The FBI experts quickly run all possible alphabet combination again and many words came out. Having some 17,500 words start with alpha D and over 990 words start with alpha V, you know how many word combinations that will result in? The FBI uses their amazingly fast computers and quickly come up with the suspect "DronaVirus", but what does it mean? You the reader are smart and found it before our FBI did. Does it mean they plan to spread the virus using drones? Can it even be done? Viruses are not alive and very quickly they can become inactive so how could Chima maintain them as active in drones? Easy…have them cooled, maybe. Have they used a special protein to cover them and then uncover the protein with special chemicals or enzymes in the drones when needed?

TC also indicated that Chima's plan had always been to have their many labs ready for production of vaccines once they are given the necessary data and the vaccines. How many production labs? Over 2,500 smaller and bigger labs and the Chima CDC are all ready to go to mass production and vaccinate 1.3 billion people.

Now that Chima knows that Charles has finally developed the vaccines, his lab can provide the full information for mass production of the vaccines to Chima. They did not want the U.S. to have the developed vaccines, so Chima decides that Charles needs to be eliminated soon after they receive the vaccine.

Chima knows that ability to protect the future was the key in their success. Chen, who was Chima's most famous epidemiologist had books written for the government of Chima studying and providing statistical analysis to 'make a projection' as to 'what portion' of the society will get sick if and when exposed to any virus. His book clearly spelled out the most effective timing of the breakout to be the most damaging. More importantly, what blood type is more exposed to the virus, and which regions could be affected faster.

Chen's book was heavily used by Chima's strategists for a planned attack on the West, but what plan exactly? A bio attack? That is mean. If Chima already has the viruses, and if they unleash it on the world at this time without vaccinating their own citizens, everyone of their citizens will be in danger. They know that they have to work hard and fast with Charles and Chen to expedite the vaccine development and production. Chima desperately needs the suspension that contains live, attenuated, killed or modified organisms that will produce the antigen-specific antibodies.

Charles had quickly realized that the five viruses work on humans so differently and with devastating effect. One attacks the immune system, one attacks the pulmonary system and can be aerosolized, one disables the absorption system, another one invades the operation of muscular systems, and the worst one is the one that attacks the neurons...like the mad cow effect of prions. The one that can be aerosolized, however is the fastest one to spread.

Now let's Quantum Jump and go to the DA's office and see what is going on. We have not been there for some time.

"Guys, we have another mystery added to our case. The result of the latest rerun of the DNA database shows that there is a third brother to Buzz and Innocenti. The blood matches perfectly with this third brother, Charles Alvin. The DNA's nucleotides matches with Charles more precisely than with the DNA of Innocenti or Buzz. We asked the database manager, Li C. Chang, how in the world this DNA was previously missed to be identified with Charles. We were told that when the DNA database was originally run for matching, the backed-up data that was used had been corrupted. Now, with their latest software, they have rerun the matching and synched all DNA databases and backups. An insane explanation, but it is what it is. We don't know why and how this happened. They suspect foreign agents may have been involved and the FBI is analyzing this...if they have time to get away from party politics of course. They are suggesting the database manager, Li C. Chang to be fired," the DA said.

Now the FBI must talk to the new suspect, Charles. They call and ask him to come in with his attorney. Sitting with his attorney, the FBI interrogates Charles with tough questions and finally takes the case to another Grand Jury. After a week, the FBI comes to Charles' lab and puts him under arrest...but what for? Was it for working to find the vaccine for the five viruses for the enemy or was it for money laundering? Heck no! It is for the murder of Anna. But how did they find out about Charles' involvement with that murder? Was it the Tycho connection? Did he somehow know something about the murder? Did Chen inform the FBI or what is going on here? The FBI is still puzzled and are analyzing the mystery case, and we know how long that will be!

Charles has no choice but to tell the FBI about the vaccination and his suspicion of the potential use of the viruses to attack the U.S. We don't know if he has already given the final vaccine information or different kinds of live vaccines to Chen, and therefore to the Chimese Communist country for mass production. The news of Charles' arrest gets to Chen and to Chima. Now the government of Chima gets nervous as to what Charles is going to tell or give to the U.S. government.

If we apply what Buzz was saying in that debate about Prayers, we can't pray for our own country anymore, we are sure the Chinese are praying for their country as well. God is now put in an awful situation. Whose prayers should he listen to? Ours, with a population of some 328 million…or 1.3 billion Chinese? You and I did not create this Universe, so we should let god suffer and decide and choose who to kill!

Apparently Chima, through their agents, had been planning for this for a long time to have Charles framed in some ways. Chima had established, through their agents, so much control over drone manufacturing and computer software in the United States. They are ready to implement their plan in ten major cities. They also had internal control over other companies that are producers of major telecommunication software, hardware, consumer electronics, and smartphones. They had their agents…men and women in trucking companies, slaughterhouses and chicken farms. This is for the delivery of the viruses. Was this ten the same 10 that TC was referring to? Now Chima must act quickly.

The FBI urgently goes to find TC, but he has gone to Chima. When will he come back? Had Chima planted the blood and skin of Charles at the murder scene by hiring someone to kill the head of the World Bank…someone famous for publicity and Anna was killed by mistake? We can only guess that Chima wanted to have a threat over the head of Charles and with the threat of conviction to get him to produce and deliver the vaccines. But why Charles amongst millions of people? Well, he had his lab and they needed his expertise.

Back to our informer TC. He is back and quickly giving another piece of information to the FBI. He gives them the video he had promised to bring from Chima. This is the actual recording of the killing of Anna and informs them how it was planned and implemented.

The video very clearly shows the killing. Innocenti and Charles are not the murderers, so who is? A Chimese man, who fled the scene, is clearly shown on the video. Charles is not the killer and he now is a free man. And now the U.S. needs his expertise. Innocenti's charges are dropped as well. They all celebrate, finally relieved.

One day Charles was sitting with Elon and the telephone rings. Charles picks up, with a "Hello?"

"Hey, Charles...this is Innocenti...your patient. I have not seen you Doc for some time, and I need to come see you," Innocenti explained

"Why don't you come to my house now if you have nothing else to do. I will text you my address," Charles said.

"Ok I will. I hope you don't mind if I bring my brother Buzz with me?" Innocenti asked.

"Oh no, bring *our* brother with you. I know he looks just like you," Charles said.

Innocenti was surprised by Charles referring to "our brother" and that he knew Buzz looked like Innocenti, but he made his way to see Charles at his house.

Charles opens the door and as soon as he sees Innocenti with Buzz he pauses for a second. He jumps and hugs his two brothers. They celebrate with passion. Scotty and Marsha had told Charles the whole story about his other brothers. Now the family is all united. Everyone shares their story. Charles told them that they should go and surprise Scotty and Marsha, as he had been there before many times. They drive up to the mountain top property and saw a big sign:

"City of 'BayDana' Population 2, Enter at Your Own Risk"

Buzz and Innocenti went ahead toward the house. Charles was hiding behind a big stone and just watching. They notice a man and a woman tending their vegetable garden, the man eating a cucumber. What a feeling. For the first time they are meeting their biological parents. Scotty and Marsha are first scared a bit seeing two strangers as no stranger had ever come to their property.

"Hello guys...ugh...what can we do for you?" Scotty says, holding a defensive posture with his shovel.

"Hello…we are not here to hurt or bother you sir, so please relax," Buzz said.

"Oh no, I am a strong tough guy…and not afraid of anyone any way. What can we do for you two?" Scotty says.

"The fact that we look alike may tell you something, does it not? Can you guess who we are? Were we born here?" Buzz asked, with a sly smile.

Following suite, Innocenti added, "Do you think we may be twins?"

Marsha realizes what is going on and jumps to her boys and gives them big hugs and kisses. We are so happy to have seen you…my boys!"

How did you find us?" Scotty asked, in tears.

"Well that was fairly easy. Charles told us," Innocenti answered.

"Charles?" Scotty asks surprised.

Charles comes to the group laughing. Then Marsha and Scotty realized what had happened and began laughing with them. They all celebrated with Scotty and Marsha. For them, there were no differences whatsoever between biological and their adoptive parents and there were no bitter feelings towards Marsha or Scotty.

The following week, to celebrate his freedom, Charles goes with Elon to his beach house in Florida. As he was sailing with Elon, and the two were deep sea fishing, another boat approached them, a few strong men came on board. They took Charles by force to their fast boat, set Charles' boat on fire, and threw Elon into the ocean. Elon is worried about his Dad and he, himself is in danger of drowning. He somehow manages to swim to the shore in the shark infested ocean. He goes to the police and reports the incident. Charles has been kidnapped by the men on the boat. They take him to Chima through other smaller countries, and upon entrance at the airport he is arrested for espionage. Now the U.S. is more nervous.

Chima charged Charles for espionage against the People's Republic of Chima. He is on TV as the reporters state that his international goal was to destroy one billion Chinese residents. He is jailed and his sentence is the Death Penalty, with two years reprieve. Under this kind of sentence under Chinese law, the sentence of the prisoner can only be reduced from death penalty to life…and only if he makes great contribution to the society. The only way for him to be pardoned is if Chima's Committee of the National People's Congress makes a different decision and if Chima's President signs off on it. Since he was still needed by Chima the president signs the order right away, but only under the condition that he stays in Chima to work on the vaccine. They rush the process because of their need.

Now we take a slight Quantum Jump to catch up with Anna's brother-in-law, who as a drug lord. He has a massive network worldwide and knows about Charles being in Chima. His imbedded agents had mentioned that the database showed that Charles' blood had been found at the murder scene. He must take revenge for Anna, not knowing the fact that Charles was not the killer and has been cleared of all charges on the killing of Anna. Revenge is the only thing going around in his brain. He also has to take revenge for Jose Rodriguez being jailed after kidnapping of Innocenti. He has two choices: have one of their band members kill Charles or bring him back to their 'court of justice'. He chooses the latter. After all, we have seen the drug lords massive network and miles of tunnels under the most secured U.S. jails to rescue one of their own. They can do anything they want…even in Chima!

The network of these drug lords breaks into the toughest security barriers. His network agents know how their Chinese networks work. Apparently they had more agents in Chima than the U.S. government did! They kidnap Charles and bring him back to the U.S. through Mexico. They will arrange the same court that they had for Innocenti. We now know what had happened to Innocenti in this court, but this time they want to make sure that Charles is convicted and killed. The Chinese government is bewildered. Where is Charles? Have the U.S. agents killed him to prevent Chima from achieving their goal of coming up with the vaccine? Or has he been taken back to the United States?

Elon and Charles' parents are all sad and depressed. Our poor Charles goes through the same court procedure that his brother Innocenti went through but right before his execution Anna's brother-in-law gets the report from their own network agents about who had killed their daughter. No revenge on Charles. Charles is released and given apologies. He is blind folded and released in an abandoned building. Did the drug lords have agents implanted within the FBI and saw the video? Probably so.

Charles and Elon are now in protected custody by the U.S. government. They don't want another kidnapping. Charles knew that each protein in the virus has a specific bio scent, just like the unique bio scent of an egg, for example. With his background in engineering, biology and specialty in making small gadgets, he had already made thousands of such gadgets to find anyone who is infected with the five viruses. The U.S. government orders a massive amount of these gadgets, as well as millions of masks to be produced…just in case.

Charles also has good connections to many dog breeders with whom he had worked. The special dogs were quickly trained, specifically to find these five bio scents. The news comes to the FBI with reports that Chima, during Charles' absence, had stolen all the information they needed from his lab and had already transferred some developed vaccines to Chima. All they need is time to mass produce the vaccines. Charles' data on vaccine production is mostly destroyed.

Within weeks, Chima is using their labs to go into rapid action and very quickly mass produces the vaccines and vaccinates their people. They are now fully ready to start the bio assault on the West.

Why are we, as Americans so worried about the communist country of Chima? They love us, don't they? We all know that when we download many software programs, we should not have any doubt that Chima will be the "guest of honor" in our house, bedroom, kitchen, and in our home office computer. You know why? Because they have a very caring government. The damn Communist Party wants to see how we cook, what we talk about, and what is going on in our bedrooms, so they can help us…have no doubt about that. Chima really cares about us and loves us all so dearly. They care about our wellbeing!! Right! But they also want to attack us with five unknown dangerous viruses. You figure.

Another Quantum Jump. The day has come. The bio assault starts.

The Communist Party, with their 1,500 strategists and the Chima's Liberation Army and military leaders are monitoring and directing the Shock and BioAwe. The order goes to all agents.

The attack starts with their 10,000 human carrier Hara-kiri or Seppuku, unknown to the west. They are boarded in various airlines, headed for the west. They start spreading the most dangerous of all five viruses, the virus VR2SFTCP. This is the one that can be aerosolized. The Chinese government had selected the Hara-kiri agents from people who did not look Chinese, as to not even raise any suspicion of the western homeland security system.

At the same time, the DronaVirus planes start spreading the viruses in ten major cities, selecting the most populous cities in the U.S. and many others in Europe. Other DronaVirus planes go over the selected U.S. ships and spread the same viruses on them. Those drones that attacked the ships are all downed by the incredibly happy U.S. forces as they celebrate their downing. But it is too late…the job is done. The sailors get sick, one at a time.

The Chimese agents had located many truck stations and start their spreading of VR2SFTCP among truck drivers. Their plan was to paralyze food and other products distribution system. Mice and rats are released by other agents to spread the other four viruses, in accordance with the master plan. The mice were injected right before they go to the slaughterhouses and chicken farms. Detailed reports constantly go to Chima for monitoring and to receive directions and orders.

Chima had previously set up their 10G servers and other equipment in special locations inside the U.S. and in their many satellites. All were repositioned and ready to take charge in case the U.S. attacks Chima's military. But they had not started their operation until now. They take over the communication network and overwhelm the slower 5G network. Their almost fully unpredictable Random Bit Generator jamming devices started their work to disengage the slower networks like 5G, they are not able to compete with the speed of the 10G servers.

The U.S. is in trouble, and so are many of the European countries. All Chima needs to do is just wait and watch. Nobody can blame Chima…their hands are so called 'clean.' How can you prove that it was Chima who implemented this plan? After all, viruses are created naturally in the animal kingdom and have been for millions of years. Their friendly Allies ignore so much evidence produced by the Western countries. The countries that believe in Chima's denial won't even consider the evidence. At this point, Chima does not even care if they are blamed since their mission is 99% complete. All they must do is watch and wait for their predicted downfall of the West, something that has been the Communist Party's intent for decades.

The communications system in the U.S. goes down. A few of the satellites are hit and damaged by Rubbas and Chima causing all sorts of domino effect. Cellphones, banking, gas and food distributions are all in trouble. The stock market goes down ninety five percent overnight. The healthcare system is in shambles as all hospitals are full and cannot accept new patients. Death rates quickly jump to 40,000 people a day, just in the United States. Unemployment goes up to eighty percent within a few days. The banking system is all messed up. Chinese hackers were all fully engaged, now many of them are using the 10G network.

But is Chima safe?

Chima now has complete control over the vaccine and they already have their own people vaccinated so they are not worried about any major death of their own people. But should they worry? They had tested the vaccine on 900 people who were selected. Chen and Charles had selected them as potential recipients in their human trials. At the time they had tested it, the results were successful, and all patients had recovered. Chima notices that many people still get sick with the symptoms related to the viruses. How though? They quickly arrest and control anyone who is sick. Not many…just about 90,000 Chimese.

What Chima did not know was that Charles and Chen had played their smart hand on Chima, finding that the vaccines worked only on about one percent of the people with blood types O negative, A negative, B negative, and AB negative. This is only an extremely low percentage of the Chinese people. When Chen was told to test the vaccine on Chinese people, in collaboration with Charles, they used the Chinese blood database and selected 900 people, supposedly random. They were actually selected carefully by Chen to pick the candidates with only these blood types. Chen and Charles were not sure about the intent of the communist Chinese government and this was their insurance policy.

Now Chima is in trouble with the rest of the world. Charles provides the vaccine production information to the U.S. labs and they quickly start mass producing with full speed. Suddenly many explosions happen in many of the major vaccine production facilities in the United States, for reasons unknown. Is this the "Power of Agency" that the defectors were talking about? The power of having imbedded agents in the United States.

Chima again has control over the vaccine production. Now having the information needed from Charles and his lab, Chima quickly develops the vaccine that works on all blood types and against the five vaccines. Chima takes credit for that and gives the vaccine to all their friendly countries, but not to any western style governed countries, democracy is now in trouble. Chima takes over the oil fields of the Middle East. Rubbas turns off the Gas pipe to Europe.

In two weeks, the estimated death counts goes to 300 million in the western countries. Chima has an adequate amount of vaccines for the world and the western countries have no choice but to accept a long-term contract with Chima to get the vaccine. The price was for the U.S. and their Allies to give up control of their nuclear arsenals and many of the military bases and submarines to the Chinese government. The western countries are replaced by other countries in the United Nations and lose their voting power in the Security Council, Economic and Social Council, and the International Court of Justice. Pretty much all their power is submitted to Chima and their allies.

The President of the United States, the head of the European countries, Japan, Israel, Canada and Australia sign the surrender declaration and hand it over to the President of Chima in a broadcasted ceremony held in Chima's capital city. The western countries are now in depression and the Chinese government announces a new world order. The dollar is replaced by the new Chinese money and the rest is history.

The whole world is changed. When will it change again? Who knows? Maybe Elon knows. When and how will he tell us? Hopefully soon.

Charles was unfortunately killed in a car accident in Washington DC, hitting another car coming from the side going through a red light. The driver was Mr. Zan Zan, who fled the scene and was not found to be charged. The U.S. authorities are still looking for him. The accident caused a big fire and Charles was charred as he became unconscious after the accident.

When the news gets to his boy Elon, he was devastated. Now his love was also gone in the same way his biological parents were gone. He plans revenge, but without a drop of blood to be shed.

Charles' body was given to his adoptive parents who agreed to give his remains to Scotty and Marsha. Everyone is much older now. Charles gets buried on the mountain top property where he was born. Poor Charles experienced his Hell here on Earth, twice. Rest in Peace Charles.

Elon did not move to the mountain top property but kept a close relationship with all the family. He became a very tough and strong man, following in the steps of Charles by taking over his lab, as per Charles' will. He resurrected the lab, almost to its original capabilities. He made one promise as Charles was being buried.

"Chinese people are nice and caring people," Elon said, crying. "I won't take revenge, even from their communist party, but you will see how the U.S.A. will resurrect itself again. I know how...you showed me how, Dad...

and I will accomplish that for your soul. I will continue your path and I will make this world a peaceful place. Yes Dad, you told me that 'our flaws are biological, and the solution should also be biological,' and you showed me how. I have your skin, your DNA, and I promise I will bring you back…I have no doubt. Rest in peace, my caring Dad," said Elon, with great care. We don't know how he will resurrect the U.S.A. Maybe we will find out soon, as he promised not to do it in a revengeful way. Good luck, Elon. We will read his book…or better to say we will see the result of it soon.

Reading a few pages of Charles' book, which was dedicated to his parents and Elon, showed how caring he was and what his plan was for the Red Planets to become Blue Planets. He hated the killing in our biological beings. His only focus was peace for the world. His sole goal was to be able to remove human aggression from their brains by using the neuronal circuits and network that he had developed. The network that he had planted in Innocenti's brain.

Charles' intention and beliefs were all very clearly written in his published book, Changing all Red Planets to Blue, and in another book with the title,

Nine 11, Why 11, Mine 11, None 11.

Well after all of this should we even care to unravel the mystery of who killed Anna? Millions killed, and unfortunately we could not prevent it. We failed.

But how did Chima plan for the killing and how did they execute it? It is about time that we unravel the mystery…the killing of Anna Rodriguez. We promised to find our mystery killer, but sometimes it is a system that does the killing. Was the murderer in this case another country? Who in that country? We now know that it was a person used by another country to kill Anna. We found the exact person who committed the actual murder of Anna Rodriguez.

Sometimes when a person is killed, like in this case Anna, you have to look at the reasons behind the scenes and make projections for the future. Who else will die or be killed? Maybe thousands, hundreds of thousands, or millions. We should not be satisfied with finding the killer of Anna. This is the only way you prepare your own system to prevent wars from happening. All countries should, for our human species.

So, let's review a summary of what Chima had planned and how they implemented their evil plan, even though you, as a smart reader, have almost fig-ured it out already. Chima wanted to rule the world, so they assembled the biggest strategists and scientists to plan and accomplish this. They had a strong military, but their final decision was to have a bio attack on the West. They lacked bio capability, so they needed help. They looked for the best lab and scientist in the world. They find Charles and his lab. They can pay or bribe him, but they can frame him for a murder, that way they will have an insurance policy just in case he does not deliver. Then he can be pushed with disclosing the murder he 'committed'.

The plan started way back before Anna is killed, when they get Charles involved in a fake accident in Chima and kept his blood and skin growing in special medium. Because they had their agent imbedded and responsible for the U.S. DNA database management, they already knew he had two other brothers. They had analyzed the database and had noticed that three DNA strands matched exactly…one of them was Charles. The plan was set, but how can they implement this? They select the victim, the head of the World Bank, and have the person commit the murder. They do not want to blame it on Charles yet because they need to have time for the development of the vaccine, and they must have time to manipulate the DNA database. To buy time, they first blame the brothers. The closest DNA to Charles' is that of Buzz, but since he is orbiting the earth at the time of the murder, the closest match must be Innocenti's blood. Naturally Innocenti will be blamed. Charles' DNA was excluded from the DNA data pool by the Chimese agent. Going through the whole process of convicting Innocenti gives Chima adequate time for the development of the vaccine.

They hire a killer to take out the head of the World Bank, but Anna gets killed by mistake. Charles' freshly kept blood and skin is spread at the scene. Chima had many agents imbedded where the United States stores the DNA database, so the agent could manipulate the database any day, depending on who was to be blamed.

The day of the murder the killer had made excellent cover to look normal, like a jogger. He had five stolen cars located in strategic places to get away and not be tracked. After committing the murder, he put the fresh blood and skin of Charles over the body and in the area surrounding it and fled the scene. He had a self-recording camera on his head and recorded the whole thing. Why did he do that? Because he was a serial killer and has been keeping his collection in Chima. He enjoyed reviewing them. Sick. God's creation or natural selection?

Chima had selected the best agent…one who enjoys killing. Anna is murdered… really not by this killer, but by a system…by the Communist Party of Chima.

Mrs. Fragrant was a Chimese agent who had asked Innocenti to come to that city on that day. She had Innocenti's blood and skin and she spread both his blood and skin around Anna's body, now Charles' blood and Innocenti's can be found on Anna's body. So Innocenti gets convicted. All of this is giving time to Chima to have the vaccine developed and delivered. Then once the vaccines are delivered, they are done with Charles and he can now be convicted or killed. How? They change the DNA database and put in the samples to run and identify him as the most matching DNA by his blood and skin. They report the finding to the FBI. Mrs. Fragrant was convicted as a Chimese agent and is in jail.

Well, we lost…but the Universal process has its way to bring the U.S. back. When? We don't know.

Chapter 12
Back to the Mountain Top, The Dream

Innocenti, Maria, Buzz, and Mary all move to the mountaintop property and build their own log homes, living a happier life with Scotty and Marsha. They also build two bigger log homes for their adoptive parents who move in as well. This was a way for Innocenti and Buzz to show their appreciation for them…there were no differences of love between their adoptive and biological parents. They are all in a safer place now.

One afternoon, everyone is present and are having coffee in the yard enjoying the nice spring weather. Mary and Maria were whispering something for a few minutes. Everyone's attention was on them.

"What are they talking about?" Innocenti asked.

"I don't know, maybe one of those women's talk?" Buzz answered.

Well Mary and Maria came and joined the group and had their coffee. They had coordinated a statement together and started singing it at the same time with a nice rhyme.

> "Who knows God may have given us a Triplett,
> If so, we will call them Scarlett, Albert and Collett
> If they turned out to be twin
> You can call them Kevin and Gwynn
> If we are not lucky and only one
> That will make it easy, you can call him Cameron
> Mary and Maria together said…
> We have not had our period for two months…,"

Scotty and Marsha wanted them to have triplets so they both said…

Let it be Triplett…Scarlett, Albert and Collett,"

Now let's do our last Quantum Jump and go the author's house, Ben, who has been sleeping and dreaming.

"Wake up Ben, wake up,"

Ben's wife wakes him but sweetly shaking him and saying, "You crazy man, you have been dreaming and talking like crazy. Go take a shower, you stinky man. Your shirt is all soaked from sweating. Go right now. You have been screaming, laughing and talking like crazy. We did not want to wake you up, because with our children and granddaughter around we were watching you and we said, 'why should we wake him up? This is like the best movie in action. Let his movie play to the end and finish'. It was the best movie we have ever watched. You were explaining it all in detail, we are glad that it was only a dream,"

Ben's daughter joins in and said, "I'm telling you he has gone crazy,"

Ben's son asked, "Who had written the story?"

Ben's granddaughter said, "The Universe?"

Ben's wife said, "He always talks crazy about the Universe, God, and how we got here…and why we do what we do…and whether we have Freewill or not. You should read his crazy upcoming books on these subjects. Telling you, my kids…your Dad has gone crrrrraaazy. We are happy that you are alive. Go take a shower right now, you stinky man," She finished.

Ben was finally coming out of his crazy dream, but for him it was not crazy. He tells them he loves them and how concerned he is about them and his adopted country, the U.S.A. and the world. He is now in the shower singing. His wife and children all are now spying on him by listening as he sings his favorite song…."on the road again…."

"God he has such an awful voice," The granddaughter says.

Everybody confirms.

"But it comes from his heart…or as he always used to tell me…trillions and trillions and trillions of his proteins are moving and synching to make the song coming from his vocal cords," Ben's wife said. "But such a nice scent coming from his shower. He must have been using his own developed AlcoSoap! Let him finish his song," She urges.

"Hey Dad, should we take you to one of these mental rehab places," His son asks jokingly.

"Who me?" Ben asks. "Heck no! Maybe they should take *all of you* to a mental institution. I don't think there will be any hope for Y'all anyway," Ben jokingly says.

The End or the Beginning? There is no start and there is no end. But even if such a start and end did exist, we are just our crazy Universe playing the fiddle of life, all in the middle.

Chapter 13

Conclusive Remarks

A Summation of the Living You.

We have reached the end of the book, but not the end of the stories of our lives. I hope that you enjoyed the journey with me. Yes, it is a strange world… has been and will ever be…at least for the living with the constant pushing and pulling of the non-living. Life is strange, very strange!

The story I shared was thrilling. Even though it was a science fiction, it had some real-life episodes that were weaved into a fictional story. Some of the characters that we encountered may have been real life characters…some good people and some bad, some downright nasty, some kind, and some evil. Most importantly, our story was about how loving, mean, and dangerous the Human Species can potentially be. The book tried to show how fragile the foundation of our country's economy and security system is. All that is needed to destroy it are a few viruses.

Did we obtain Justice by finding the killer? Even the world did not. But did we *really* achieve justice in our much larger theatre of collective lives? Justice is a huge word and achieving it is not easy. When you put a person in a court room and do your best to bring justice to the victim, your limited access to all information prohibits you to reach the real goal of what we call "Justice."

When a person commits a crime, it is not just him that needs to be tried… maybe his parents, his friends, his teachers and the whole society with all its shortcomings have to be on trial. Maybe the country, all nations and our Universe. And if there is a creator he, or she, or it should be on trial.

As our fictional character Charles said, the problem is biological, and the solution will eventually have to be biological, if possible. The solution won't be religion based. It cannot be. If the religion is just a "Summon to Action" then we should not complain. We have seen how each person or a sect or a country reads that "Summon to Action" so differently and acts on it in different ways. We have seen the beheadings, the bombings, the theft and the rapes. The reaction of all countries taking revenge. Has it solved anything for the human species?

I do not see a golden rule, if ever there is one, it is our changing and evolving DNA. In any complex system many more things can go "wrong" and it is just a function of applied probabilities. We know that our DNA and our brains are the most complex entities in our known Universe, so we should expect many biological mishaps.

Imagine your brain with some 100 billion neurons, each having up to 10,000 branches, called dendrites, is trying to figure out what "justice" is… what "survival" is…what "good" is… and what "bad" is. Sometimes you yourself are not sure of a decision you are about to make. However, your decisions must be made in a fraction of a second. To decide, you debate it in your own brain and perform a vigorous fight in many sections of your own brain before you formed a decision…a decision which may kill or adversely affect many others. You yourself were not sure of the correctness of your decision. If you were, you would not have debated it in your brain.

If you were the only *living* creature in the world you would not even think about this kind of problem. But as a society, as a species… we do. We have no other choice but to confront it. Seven billion people with the same complex brain are doing the same thing…making decisions that affect others. Sometimes it affects millions or billions, for and against each other. The seven billion people are also trying to decide what is "good" and what is "bad." Look at this huge and complex information system that activates the collective human thought and action…sometimes in aggressive modes with wars or mass killings. Are you still surprised why countries engage in nasty wars?

Now, add to this complex brain system the epigenetic effect…the effect of what is above and beyond our genetics, which is pulling and pushing us without our knowledge…the constant effect of chemicals and radiation modifying us.

The journey of our life is a continual. We only shared a part of our journey of life…the way we were made from the universal dust, the quantum vibration of different fields, the constant conversion of energy to matter and vice versa. Our lives are only a part of a continual movie. It did not start with us when we realized we are a conscious being and it won't end with our heartbeat flattening out on the screen. We shared it in a passing and ever-changing way. A journey that between me and you will take its "separate but connected" path from hereon, but they will always be connected during our lifetime and after. We all shared and let the "stuff" we were made of communicate with each other, atom by atom, organ by organ, mind by mind, quantum field by quantum field. We shared the living side of the Universe; and we will continue sharing the stuff and the available universal energy in its vast, ever-present quantum fields.

We were never ever fixed as a "human" The "life" in us did not start when we were conceived since the sperm and the egg each already had a "life" of their own to start with. Their lives started some 3.7 billion years ago and even had representations at the moment of the Big Bang some 13.8 billion years ago…and who knows…maybe even before that. All the information needed to make you was already in those sperm and egg. With some "given genetics," we had a so-called "start," but then the epigenetic of the Universe…the chemicals, the nutrition's, the radiations…continually changed us, made us or broke us. The Universe has and will continue to discriminate. It made some of us kind and some mean…if we can call it that…against and for each of us. Why? We simply don't know but we can call it quantum probabilities…the unknown woven into what we so casually call "Freewill"

Billions of those sperms were fighting to get to the egg and millions "wasted" until the two joined to make you. You represent the winner of that first fight, if we can even call it a fight. Unfortunately, the Universe has taught us that fighting may be the only way to survive. Sad. Can it be changed? Charles and Elon thought so.

You really must absorb these statistics about your own body to appreciate who you are and how your existence evolves. You were never fixed as a "you" so there was really never a constant "You." Imagine that you have an estimated 30 trillion cells in your body, together with some 38 trillion bacteria cells that are in or over your body, each coexisting and living together so peacefully, and sometimes not so peacefully. Each one of these cells "exchange" and "transact" with the Universe

billions of times every fraction of a second. They are constantly changing parts…
giving and receiving. You are changing. You become a "Weighted Rolling Average"
of the changing you, never fixed but constantly being modified. You only imagined
yourself as a "fixed" and constant "You" because of this averaging and the average
information that stayed in your cells…especially your neurons in your brain…
your memory. Because these changes are so nanoscopic, you don't feel the change,
but the average is constantly changing, without you "knowing".

These are just the cells in your ever-changing body, but now consider the
fact that each of these cells are made of millions of three-dimensional chemical
units we call proteins. Consider the fact that each one of the 100 trillion cells
of your body are made up of millions of proteins, and if those proteins won't
move or change shape then you won't move, talk, or think. The proteins only
change shape with positive or negative electrical or ionic charges. We should
wonder how in the world trillions and trillions of these proteins change shape
in a "synchronized way" for you to talk, walk, and even think.

This is an amazing wonderland of ever-changing and ever forming "You"
and "Me," We should cherish it, even if we don't fully understand the ultimate
source of its energy. The vibration, oscillation, the periodicity, the pressure, the
constant tuning, turning…and ultimately the pattern of movement, is not the
wonder of the Universe, but it is "our" wonder. Put it all together and we see
that us, as human beings, are a part of it. We contribute to it and change it as it
changes us. It gives us pleasure or pain in the process. Only if you cherish this,
can you bring pleasure and understanding into your pain in this relational world.

The periodic pumping of the heart, the oscillation of your lungs, the magnificent vibration of your voice cords is all just the tip of the iceberg in the living
you. Just see how trillions of proteins have to "synchronize in real time" on the
top of your tongue and your vocal cords to so delicately vibrate and control the
airflow from your lungs to produce a loving or hateful word, to talk or sing.
They have to synchronize for you to create the exact wavelength and frequency
needed when your brain tells you to bring your voice down so your child's sleep
won't be disturbed, you care. Whether the patterns are simple or complicated
does not matter…it is the wholesomeness of it all that makes the changes in you,
in this wonderland of Spacetime we call our Universe.

As we can never tell when life started, we also have difficulty telling when
we die. I saw the last breath of my father. As I was watching the screen monitor

that showed his heart rate, I noticed the heartbeat went down to eight and then up to eighty and then to zero......a flat line_____. Was he dead or still alive and just not responding? His cells were not dead yet, and until his last cell so called, "died" he was still alive in a way.

We have such complexity imposing itself on our decision-making process. Decisions about our own psyche, God, family, friends, city, nation and other nations. We know one thing and that is that our decision affects others and the decision of others affect us. So the only thing we *can* do is to do our best to be "good" to others, to be "kind," to be "productive," to "love others," and to "share our resources" Knowing that, in this vast process and we are only doing our best with the information system built into our cells acting the way they do. Know that your mistakes are most probably God's, or "Godia's" mistakes to have created us to make the decision we make. Freewill or not does not matter once we realize the wholesomeness of the world. Freewill is only to satisfy ourselves to write laws and to punish the "wrong dear", and to supposedly streamline our society without paying much attention to the real causes of issues. We will do what we will do, whether we believe in freewill or not, and therefore Freewill becomes somewhat an evolving irrelevance.

We should never forget that for each winner there is a loser. Winning and losing unfortunately do not neutralize each other. One causes satisfaction and the other causes displeasure and pain. But does the real Universe give a damn? It continues its course until its energy runs out, if it ever will.

This whole process reminds us of the news anchor Walter Cronkite, when at the end of his nightly news report he would say, "and that's the way it is".

In nature, we are at home and nature is at home in us. It is the wholesomeness of it all. It is this wholesomeness that can never be separated. It is a connected wholesome. It is our connected "Relational Universe". Our joy or hatred comes to "realization" when the Outness connects with our Inness and the Quantum Probabilities puts its bet on either one, or both at the same time.

Your intention and mine is to help leave a better viable world. I have no doubt that all of us will do our best to make that a reality to our dying days. Let's hope that the decisions of the collective mind of "human species" is always based on Love and not Hatred. Impossible, but who knows if Elon will succeed in his "biological" attempt.

Chapter 14
Back to the "City of BayDana"

You have been my Pal reading this book, so let's jointly do something very strange and unusual. Let's go visit some of the characters of our book and introduce ourselves to them. I will introduce myself as the writer, Ben Compani, and you introduce yourself with your name as the reader. We will start with Scotty and Marsha and take it from there. So, let us move to the City of Bay-Dana. Here we see Scotty and Marsha, tending to their vegetable garden. I will go first, and you follow me. Here we go.

Hello Scotty, Hi Marsha…thank you for letting us come and see you. It has been a pleasure. I am Ben Compani and here is my pal_____.

Neither one of you know me or my Pal. You have no idea who we are, but we know exactly who you are. We "created" you, we assigned you different good and bad traits and characters. We gave you "life", we moved you around, and let you have friends and foes. You were all under our control, you had no will of your own. We even forced you to quit your jobs and go on to your mountain top property. We forced you to have children…you lucky couples…they turned out to be triplets.

We made Innocenti a bit confused, but Godly. We made Buzz and Charles two smart scientists. We gave Elon a good amount of self-confidence, but we should have asked him to be a little humbler.

We forced you to give them up for adoption. Had we decided for you to raise them on your own, our story would have turned out to be totally different. Therefore our brain would have formed so differently, and in our daily physical lives and movements would have taken other alternative routes. You changed us more than we changed you.

175

Isn't this the way the world has been and continues to form and shape our fate, moving us around most of the time without any will on our part controlling it? As we were moving, we were being curved and we were curving the space, we were getting or losing our masses.

The nature or a creator created me and my pal the same way. We were created by all forces of the Universe, 17 quantum fields or more, vibrating in Spacetime, and not by telling our parents to create us. We did not choose to be here, but here we are for the moment.

Hey Scotty and Marsha, you were made out of energy in a condensed form, and so were we. Sorry that we had to kill Charles, but Elon is working on that to bring him back to see you again. Maybe soon, in another paper. Poor Innocenti…we put him through hell in two different trials, but we are happy that he was not the killer. By the way, what was Buzz doing ten miles away from the Space Shuttle, he never told us. We could have forced him to tell us, but we chose not to. Did BCASSO© pay Innocenti the million dollars extra or did he back off? We never saw the money in Innocenti's account. Maybe the attorneys are suing him to pay the balance on his account.

You became a part of the epigenetic of me and my Pal reader. As we were creating you, or reading about you, you were also creating us at the same time. You were changing us as we were changing you. You created new neuronal networks in both of us. You have become a part of our lives and memory… probably forever. Hopefully one day humans much smarter than Buzz and Charles will find out how quantum theory and gravity will merge to give us a Theory of Everything. But for now, let us hope that the human species will become more loving and get rid of their aggression and hate. As Innocenti used to do, let us pray for the loving people of Chima and the USA. They can be friends. I hope Chimese people read my book as well.

"Elon" is sending his love to each one of you but reminds us that "There is no sound of one hand clapping in our Universe. There cannot be a Ping Pong unless there are two players and a stage. You give a Ping to the Universe and the Universe will give you a Pong back in return, all in a stage with interaction of forces playing it in curved Spacetime, hopefully a "Wholesome One." Sometimes it is the Universe that determines the angles you hit your Ping, based on the angle you receive the Universal Pong. It is the dance of all quantum fields that makes all sorts of patterns, us.

Let's us hope and "pray" that these Pings and Pongs are all based on love and not hate…especially between the United States of America and Chima. Chimese people and Americans should be close friends not enemies.

Whether this is our Goodbye or Hello…you decide…but I hope to see you soon, on another paper.

Goodbye for now.

ACKNOWLEDGEMENTS

Writing a book is not possible without the huge amount of knowledge you learn and obtain from the world, from the courses you take, the books you read, the sacrifices that all scientists had made for centuries to make us aware of our Universe and how our biology works, the article and books you read, many not mentioned here. The knowledge you learn from family and friends, and from the articles on the internet.

My special thanks to my two brothers and sister, they are all have studied science and have scientific minds, I have learned so much from them.

My thanks also goes to my dear editor, Christina Jillian Compani

A NOTE ON RESOURCES, NAMES AND MUST READ BOOKS

THE SOCIETY OF GENES, BY ITAI YANAI AND MARTIN LERCHER

THE ORDER OF TIME, BY CARLO ROVELLI

SEVEN BRIEF LESSONS ON PHYSICS, BY CARLO ROVELLI

FREEWILL, BY SAM HARRIS

FREEDOM EVOLVES, BY DANIEL C. DENNETT

CONSCIOUS, BY ANNAKA HARRIS

HOW PHYSICS MAKES US FREE, BY J.T. ISMAEL

TO CATCH A SPY, BY JAMES M. OLSON

ACTIVE DEFENSE, BY M. TAYLOR FRAVEL

QUANTUM SPACE, BY JIM BAGGOTT

A BRIEF HISTORY OF TIME, BY STEPHEN HAWKING

BLACK WAVE, BY KIM GHATTAS

REALITY IS NOT WHAT IT SEEMS, BY CARLO ROVELLI

CHINESE COMMUNIST ESPIONAGE, BY PETER MATTIS AND MATHEW BRAZIL

HACKING DARWIN, BY JAMIE METZL

DNA IS NOT DESTINY, BY STEVEN J. HEINE

TIME, LOVE, AND MEMORY, BY JONATHAN WEINER

THE EQUATIONS OF LIFE, BY CHARLES S COCKELL

SOMETHING DEEPLY HIDDEN, BY SEAN CARROLL

BEHAVE, BY ROBERT M. SAPOLSKY

THIS IS YOUR BRAIN ON PARASITES, BY KATHLEEN McAULIFFE

THE LANGUAGE OF GOD, BY FRANCIS S. COLLINS

THE GOD DELUSION, BY RICHARD DAWKINS

MAN'S SEARCH FOR MEANING, BY VICTOR E. FRANKL

SIGNATURE IN THE CELL, BY STEPHEN C. MEYER

HUMAN GENETICS, BY AUDIOLEARN MEDICAL CONTENT TEAM

LIFE, BY JOHN BROCKMAN

QUANTUM, BY JIM AL-KHALILI

THE EPIGENETICS EVOLUTION, BY NESSA CAREY

ORIGINS, BY NEIL deGRASSE TYSON AND DONALD GOLDSMITH

SYNCH, STEPHEN STROGATZ

INCOMPLETE NATURE, BY TERRENCE W. DEACON

THE DEEPER GENOME, BY JOHN PARRINGTON

PARALLEL WORLDS, BY MICHIO KAKU

LIFE'S RACHET, BY PETER M. HOFFMAN

STUFF MATTERS, BY MARK MIODOWNIK

INCOGNITO, THE SECRET LIFE OF THE BRAIN, BY DAVID EAGLEMAN

THE SELFISH GENE, BY RICHARD DAWKINS

THE UNIVERSE FROM NOTHING, BY LAWRENCE M. KRAUSS

WHY YOU ARE WHO YOU ARE, BY MARK LEARY, THE GREAT COURSES.

THE INTELLIGENT BRAIN, BY RICHARD J. HAIER, THE GREAT COURSES.

THERMODYNAMICS FOUR LAWS THAT MOVE THE UNIVERSE
BY JEFFERY C. GROSSMAN, THE GREAT COURSES.

FOUNDATION OF ORGANIC CHEMISTRY, BY RON B. DAVIS JR.
THE GREAT COURSES.

MANY OTHER GREAT BIOLOGY, PHYSICS AND CHEMISTRY
COURSES BY "THE GRET COURSES"

WIKEPEDIA htto://en.wikipedia.org/wiki/Penal system in China. August 17, 2020

INDEX

ABOUT THE AUTHOR

Behzad (Ben) Compani is a science lover and science writer.

He has written and has given speeches on various economics and science subjects.

His previous book published on November 5, 2012 was titled Neurolegislation, Neuro-Tax-Law and TAX STRESS

Ben is 74 years old, a member of The American Institute of Certified Public Accountant since 1981.